The Frost Haint of 'Possum Hollow and Other Tales

The Frost Haint
of 'Possum Hollow
and Other Tales

Alan Lance Andersen

Theme Park Press
www.ThemeParkPress.com

Editor: Bob McLain
Layout: Artisanal Text

ISBN 978-1-941500-76-7
Printed in the United States of America

Theme Park Press | **www.ThemeParkPress.com**
Address queries to bob@themeparkpress.com

Contents

PART ONE

TALES OF THE HOOFENGOOFERS

The Legend of Mikkelson Farm

Many years ago, before water filled the valley along the Des Moines River to make Saylorville Lake, great stands of full-growth trees stretched for mile-upon-mile of bottom land. At night, you could walk for hours among the trees by moonlight on a flat carpet of fragrant fallen leaves. This enchanted wonderland had no landmarks; nothing but the boles of cottonwood, elm, and willow trees. High overhead, the branches formed a canopy through which stars peeked down like diamonds against a black velvet sky. Moonlight gave the landscape a haunted twilight.

On a gravel road that used to run between Camp Dodge and Polk City, there was an old farmhouse hid among the trees half-way down the slope of the river valley. The house and out-buildings were weathered and run down, and the place had been abandoned for many years before the sparkling blue waters of the lake covered it over. The last people to live at the farm were an old couple by the name of George and Alma Mikkelson. They had raised a large family of children, all of whom were grown and gone by the time this story takes place.

Even at its best, Mikkelson Farm had never produced much. Most of the land was in flood plain, and the rest was on the slope that was too steep to plow. George Mikkelson had managed to support the family with a bit of farming, working as a farm hand on neighboring farms, fixing wagons and farm machinery, cutting wood, hunting, and doing mechanic work over in Polk City.

Alma Mikkelson raised chickens, tended the kitchen garden, canned vegetables, and put up pickles, jam, and preserves. She sewed clothing for her children and made warm comforters out of the rags when the clothes wore out. Alma was active in church work, always making cornstalk dolls and stocking monkeys for kids in the Blank Children's Hospital in Des Moines or for disabled children at Woodward.

When Alma was a little girl on her father's farm up by Webster City, her mother always left a bowl of milk from the family's old cow, Beulah, out at night "for the Little People". At Christmas and other holidays, Alma's mother left out cream. Uncle Charlie Owens always laughed and said it was raccoons who drank the milk, but the bowl was always empty the next morning. George and Alma Mikkelson could not afford a cow, but they carried on the tradition and left out milk from their white Saanan milkgoat, Katrina. The milk always disappeared each night.

After the Mikkelson children were grown and married, the elderly couple found it increasingly difficult to manage the farm by themselves. George had a lame back and Alma suffered from arthritis; but somehow they managed. Till one day, when he was working on Orville Seibert's tractor, George suffered a stroke that left him confined to a wheelchair unable to work.

"Now don't you fret," said Alma. "You've done fine by me all these years; now it's my turn to make us a living!"

And so she did.

But it was no easy task. Alma was by this time not just elderly — she was old. Her back was bent and her hands knobby and stiff. Still, she managed to tend the chickens and the garden, pick black raspberries in the woods in the summer, and gather walnuts in the autumn. She sold raspberry pies, rhubarb pies, squash or pumpkin pies, eggs, chickens, jams, jellies, and black walnuts. And in the springtime, she sold morel mushrooms.

Now morels are the most delicious, tender, and savory mushrooms in the world. They grow in secret places in the Iowa woodlands, and folks who know where they can be found guard that knowledge jealously. Morels are very rare, and bring high prices when you can buy them. They are seldom, if ever, available in stores. People who find them generally keep them for their own families.

Morel mushrooms like to grow near dead elm trees, and the Mikkelson Farm had acres of woodland with lots of elms. A good patch might have dozens of mushrooms; and when you pick them, new ones can spring up overnight, almost like magic. Alma knew over a dozen places where morels grew, and each spring she gathered bagfuls which she sold for more money than she made from all her pies put together.

This was back in the days before Dutch Elm Disease had wiped out one of the most beautiful of trees in the state of Iowa. Even when the elms were dead from the blight, morel mushrooms continued to grow around their skeletal trunks for several years. But eventually, as the elms rotted away, the morels ceased to grow in their accustomed places, and Alma had to wander farther and farther to find them. Finally, a year came when there were no mushrooms to be found at any of the old places, and Alma searched far up and down the river woodlands in hopes of finding a new patch.

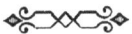

Beyond the old wooden rail fence that divided their farm from the Emhoff's, down the deep ravine, past Nelson's Creek, and into the Black Woods the old woman trudged with her empty sacks. She did not see a single morel all this way. Finally, when she was about to give up, Alma stumbled across a rocky stream that led up a gully she had never seen before. There were agates and fossils in the stream bed, and the embankments were laced with brightly colored clays — red, blue, orange, and grey — all overhung with mosses and ferns, with outcroppings of soapstone here and there.

Alma had to squeeze between two large boulders that nearly blocked the steep narrow ravine. Then the way leveled out, and she saw that the stream, now just a little babbling crick, was flowing out of a woodland glen shaped like a bowl. Springtime wildflowers carpeted the grassy bower, while ferns sprouted in the shady areas.

The source of the little crick was an artesian spring near the center of the glen, and beside it was growing the largest, most magnificent, living elm tree that Alma ever had seen in her entire life. Its trunk was as big around as a silo, and its branches towered hundreds of feet into the sky. And around the base of this elm were growing hundreds — thousands — of morel mushrooms!

Now, morels come in different sizes and colors. Some are brownish, while others are pale yellow or grey; and in this glen were all varieties. They were bigger and more succulent than any mushrooms Alma had seen before. She had only three burlap bags, and though they were large bags, there were far more mushrooms than she could ever hope to carry.

Still, there are more morels here than I've ever gathered before. I can sell these at the Farmer's Market for enough money to last till Christmas!

But then, as she started filling the first bag, Alma heard a strange, gravelly voice shout, "Here, now! Who's that stealing my mushrooms?"

Alma was startled and looked about, but did not see anyone. The voice repeated, "Who's that stealing my mushrooms?"

"I'm sorry, sir," she said, dropping the mushroom bag and wringing her hands. "Pardon me, but I didn't know they belonged to anyone, and I didn't mean to steal. I'm Mrs. Mikkelson — my farm is downriver from here."

"You're Alma Mikkelson?" the voice said. "The lady of Mikkelson Farm? You're husband's name is George and your maiden name was Owens?"

"Yes...," she said hesitantly, wondering who it was knew so much about her. Then, suddenly, Alma saw the speaker standing in the leafy bushes at the base of the great tree, half-hidden in the shadows.

It was a Hoofengoofer! He was a little man — no more than seventeen inches tall — and looked like a farmer in one of her grandmother's photographs from the 1880s. He wore a faded pair of bib overalls and a brown, high-crowned hat with a wide, floppy brim. He was frowning angrily and tugging at his long, black beard which was parted in two at the tip.

"I didn't mean to steal your mushrooms, sir," said Alma, somewhat shaken, for she had never seen a Hoofengoofer before. "I just wanted mushrooms to sell, now that my husband, George, can't work. He's had a stroke, you see. Our mushroom patches are all gone now, and when I saw these... " (The little man was staring at her with a glassy eye.) "Well, I'll just be going now. I'm sorry to have bothered you."

"Now, jist you hold on a bit!" said the Hoofengoofer. "You and yer family has been fixin' me with milk an' cream since yer Gramma's day — ever since I was a lad, and I'm a hunnerd-and-eighty-five years old!

"Now don't you fret," said he. "You've done fine by me all these years, now it's my turn to hep!"

So saying, the Hoofengoofer picked up his walking staff and knocked over a couple of dozen mushrooms with one big swipe. "You're ruining them!" cried Alma, horrified. But then she saw (with amazement) that new mushrooms was springing up in their place in the twinkling of an eye.

And what mushrooms!

These new morels were over a foot high; many of them were actually taller than the Hoofengoofer. Then the little man began filling Alma's bags with the giant mushrooms.

Oh, my! These are such fine morels, I can sell them to the supermarket manager. I'll make enough money that we'll be able to live for a whole year! We can afford to have roast beef every night — and goose every Sunday! There is enough for that...

When the bags were all full, Alma thanked the little man, who merely tugged his forelock respectfully and vanished into the woods. Alma slung the three bags over her shoulders and began trudging homeward.

Now mushrooms are not heavy, by any means. But when you have three large bags full of morels, and each mushroom is well over a foot tall and perhaps eight inches in diameter at the widest place — and when you are a very old woman with arthritis in your hands and back — you have quite a burden. But Alma toiled cheerfully down the ravine, thinking of all the fine things she could buy for herself and George.

By the time she reached the Black Woods, however, Alma was nearly exhausted. She paused to rest for a bit, but she wanted to get home before dark — and it was still a long way to go. Finally, she decided she had to leave one bag behind.

I'll still have two bags full. We can always eat chicken and eggs. I can sell these mushrooms for enough money that we'll be able to live for a good six months. We can still have roast beef on Sundays, and goose once a month. There is enough for that...

So Alma struggled onward. She made it past Nelson's Creek and toiled up the deep ravine on Emhoff's Farm. But the two bags seemed to get heavier with every step she took. When, at last, she come to her own wooden rail fence, she did not have strength enough to lift both bags over the fence, and it was still a long way through the woods to her own farmhouse. Reluctantly, she decided she would have to leave another bag behind.

I'll still have this one big bag full. We don't need to eat goose — it's much too fatty. I can sell these mushrooms for enough money that we'll be able to live for a good three months. We can still have roast beef once a month. There is enough for that...

But even the single bag seemed to get heavier and heavier. Alma could no longer carry it over her aching shoulders. Finally, she had to drag it behind her. "It's a good thing this bag is made of heavy material, or the mushrooms would be ruined," she said. "My goodness! This thing feels like it weighs more than all three bags put together did when I started."

Alma had to rest several times, sitting on a boulder or fallen log to catch her breath. Her back ached terribly and her hands could barely keep ahold of the bag. At long last she reached the farm yard, and it seemed like it took ages to make it to the kitchen door and drag the bag inside. George was sitting in his wheelchair by the cast iron woodstove.

"Where in the heck have you been?" he said. "We're nearly out of wood fer the stove..." Then he looked more closely at his exhausted wife and said, "Why, you're all done in! You better sit down, gal, and rest a bit. You're gonna kill yourself..."

"First I have to fix these mushrooms so they'll stay fresh," said Alma. "You gotta see these, George! They're the grandest morels you ever saw! I'll get some water to put them in."

As she went to fetch her grandmother's big cauldron, Alma told her husband about the strange encounter with the Hoofengoofer. George smiled in that way farmers do when their wives are talking nonsense. He wheeled his chair over to the mushroom bag while Alma filled the cauldron with water from the hand pump at the sink. She heard him gasp as he opened the bag and looked inside.

"Why, gal, you can't sell these to the supermarket and expect folks to eat 'em!" said George. It took all his strength to lift a single mushroom from the bag and hold it aloft. "Lookit this!"

Alma turned to look. The giant morel mushroom in George's trembling hand — and the others in the bag as well — had all changed into solid gold.

The old couple sold the golden mushrooms for enough money to last them the rest of their lives. They were able to buy a large new home with an oil furnace in Des Moines, to hire a cook and a housekeeper, to send all of their grandchildren to college, and to eat roast beef or goose whenever they wanted.

There was enough for that...

The Blacksmith
of Piekenbrock

A good many years ago, well before the turn of the last millennium, there was a blacksmith by the name of Otis Bickford lived out by Piekenbrock. His house was a one-room shanty; the yard with its white picket fence was decorated with flowers, whirl-a-gigs, windmills, and other whimsical things he'd fashioned out of scraps of metal and wood. Behind the house was an old shed he used as his smithy, a vegetable garden his wife Eva had planted before she died, and a twisted old pear tree that grew the best brown pears in the county.

Now with the advent of the automobile, there come to be less call for the services of a blacksmith — and Otis was too old to learn the mechanic trade like many of the other smiths did. Then come the Great Depression, and even folks with horses couldn't afford new horseshoes. Old Otis made ends meet by making toys — scale locomotives and coin banks and blacksmith puzzles of chains, rings, and bent iron — which he would take to the Farmer's Market and sell or perhaps barter for a loaf of bread and some goat's milk.

Even so, the blacksmith of Piekenbrock had a hard time of it. His neighbors said he was just too kind-hearted for his own good. A ragged little kid at the Farmer's Market would get to playing with one of his puzzles, and the blacksmith would end up giving it to her for free. Or he would be walking home afterwards and give half his loaf of bread to the friendly assortment of stray dogs that followed him everywhere he went. And each night, he would leave a bowl of warm milk and some cheese out on the oak stump by the back fence as gifts "for the Hoofengoofers".

"You're a fool, Otis Bickford!" folks would say. "You got no business giving things away when you're going hungry yourself."

But the blacksmith would just smile and say, "Well, them dogs got no one else to feed them." Or "That little tyke's mother can't afford toys, and what's childhood without toys?"

He never mentioned the Hoofengoofers.

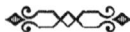

Finally one spring day came when the old blacksmith had no food at all for himself. The garden would not be producing vegetables for another month, at least, and the pear tree would not have fruit until autumn. The blacksmith didn't even have scrap metal to make toys.

It was a hungry day for him, with nothing but cold water from the pump in the back yard. It was an even longer night. He had hunger pains in his stomach, and when he finally got to sleep, he had strange dreams. Old Otis dreamed that a little man no taller than his boot stood on the bed rail at his feet and said, "Gewald Tomnoggins sends you a message. You must go to San Francisco — to the Golden Gate Bridge!"

The next day was even harder. Old Otis found a rabbit caught in his back fence, but instead of killing it for stew, he set it free. That night, the hunger pains were much worse. And the dreams were even stranger. He dreamed that three Hoofengoofers stood on the bed rail at his feet and said, "Gewald Tomnoggins is annoyed. You ignored his message. You must go to San Francisco — to the Golden Gate Bridge!"

The third day without food was the worst. The blacksmith was so weak that he didn't get out of bed. The hunger ached within him. That night, he had the strangest dream of all. The old blacksmith dreamed that his room was full of Hoofengoofers, some standing on windowsills, others on the wood stove and the kitchen table; dozens were on the floor. And on the bedpost at his feet stood Gewald Tomnoggins, the King of the

Hoofengoofers himself, wearing a tiny crown no bigger than a fat woman's bracelet.

"Otis Bickford, I'm beginning to think you're as big a fool as some folks say. You've ignored my messages. What I tell you three times is true! You must go to San Francisco — to the Golden Gate Bridge!"

A sudden breeze seemed to sweep through the room, and with a rustling sound like dry leaves caught in a whirlwind, the Hoofengoofers were gone. The old blacksmith sat shivering in his bed with the cold grey light of dawn coming through the windows. "Well, if everyone thinks I'm a fool, I may as well act like one," said Otis. He threw a few clothes into a haversack, hitchhiked into Des Moines, and hopped a freight train for California.

For the next several days, he slept in boxcars and hobo camps and ate Mulligan Stew with tramps and bums. Finally, he arrived in San Francisco and trudged wearily to the Golden Gate Bridge.

"Well, I'm here," he thought. "What do I do now?" The old blacksmith stood at the base of the bridge all day, waiting patiently with his hands in his pockets. Nothing happened.

Finally, just as the sun was setting, a man with a large mustache and wearing an apron walked up to him and said, "Say, Mister, I been watchin' you all day from my delicatessen across the way. You got me curious, and you look like you could use a sandwich. Come on over and I'll swap you some grub for your hard luck story."

The deli owner's name was Sidney Goldberg, and he sat with his elbows on the tablecloth and listened while Old Otis related his travels while eating a salami sandwich on rye with mustard and pickle and a hearty bowl of chili. When the old blacksmith told of the dream that had started his adventure, Mr. Goldberg threw back his head and laughed heartily. "Mr. Bickford, you'll pardon me for saying this, but you look exactly like the kind of looney who would chase half-way across the country because of some crazy dream! When I saw you on the bridge this morning, I said to myself, 'Sid, this guy is some kind of looney!'"

Old Otis smiled and said nothing.

The delicatessen owner went on. "It has been a pleasure to know you, my friend. But let me give you a little advice. Dreams are just crazy things in your mind. They aren't real. Why, I have dreams just as strange as yours, but I don't go traipsin' all over God's country because of them.

"Why, just last week I dreamed a little man about a foot tall was standing on my bedpost. Three nights in a row he said to me, 'Mr. Goldberg, you must go to a place called Piekenbrock. Dig under an old pear tree and you'll find a chest of treasure.' Three nights I dreamed this, but you don't see me travelling all over looking for some godforsaken Piekenbrock, as if there should be such a place. Go home, my friend, and forget about your dreams."

Old Otis Bickford went home to Iowa by the next freight train — but he did not forget his dreams. He dug under the old pear tree in his back yard, where he found a chest full of gold doubloons, bars of silver, ruby rings, and diamond necklaces. There was ancient Roman coins, sultans of Delhi, kopecks, guilders, shillings, and banknotes. Riches to last a lifetime. On the hasp of the chest was carved in ornate letters the initials 'G.T'.

The blacksmith of Piekenbrock used his treasure to build a fine new house with kennels in back for homeless or injured dogs, cats, and other animals. Each year at Christmas, he donated large quantities of toys for children of poor families. Every night, he would leave a bowl of warm milk, a loaf of bread, and a whole cheese on the old oak stump by the back fence.

And at the base of the twisted pear tree, he erected an iron statue of a little man — no taller than his boot — with a plaque that read:

Gewald Tomnoggins
King of the Hoofengoofers

Templeton Rye

Back in the days before the turn of the last millennium, there was a young feller by the name of George Darby, whose folks came from Connecticut, originally. His ma and pa died during the depression — not the Great Depression in the 1930s, but that lesser-known one back in 1920 or thereabouts. The Darby farm was sold to pay debts, and there wasn't much left over for George but his father's old Model-T truck — and it didn't work. But George was a mechanical-minded lad, and he worked on that flivver till it ran like a coyote and was quiet as an angel's prayer.

How quiet is that? Well, sir, have you ever *heard* an angel pray? There you have it.

Now this was back during the days of Prohibition, a federal program designed to help criminals help themselves by making them rich overnight. The gangsters helped themselves to a lot of money. George got a job running illegal whiskey, Templeton Rye, for a mokker in Chicago. This gangster owned a line of speakeasies all the way from Mackinaw Island to Kansas City. For those of you who aren't old enough to remember, Templeton Rye was said to be the finest of bootleg whiskey, and it was made over in Audubon County, Iowa. Initially made for local consumption, the hooch was of the highest caliber and was shipped all over the county.

Now all of this would have been fine and dandy, except for one little problem — federal agents. The G-men did their best to enforce the law, especially in Templeton. The local booze runners did all they could to avoid being caught, and the Feds did all they could to catch them. After a while, the federal men got to know and be on friendly terms with the hardest-to-catch hooch drivers. And George Darby was one of the best. His old daddy's truck wasn't the fastest, but it was dead quiet, and George knew every back road and country lane from Templeton, Iowa, to Lake Michigan. Templeton Rye sold for $5.25 or more per gallon, and Mr. Cardonna paid George $1.00 a gallon plus gasoline to drive truckloads of the stuff to his Kane County headquarters in Illinois. It wasn't enough to make George rich, but he made out fairly well.

You must understand that George Darby was not a hardened gangster — not by any means. He was a dreamy-eyed young-ster still in his teens, with more moonshine in his daydreams than he carried in his Model-T truck. He was superstitious and fanciful. He carried a rabbit's foot on his key chain, loved tall tales and ghost stories, read books on "how to interpret your dreams", and believed everything he was told. He had romantic notions about finding True Love and Buried Treasure.

Well, sir. In those days, there was a small filling station on Highway 6 down by Marion, run by an old woman called Grannie Linahen, whose husband had died some years before. George always stopped there to buy gasoline because the old lady would fix him up a sandwich and some soup to fill his stomach, and would then fill his head full of tales about bank robbers and lost silver mines while he ate. Old Grannie was also a veritable sage when it came to interpreting dreams and omens. And, when the heat was on from the G-men, she'd let George hide his truck under the haystack in her barn for a few days.

In return, George would slip the old gal a quart jar full of Templeton Rye.

Sometimes Old Grannie's granddaughter was there, too. Eunice Keller was a moonfaced girl with dark freckles on an upturned nose. She was even more of a star-dreamer than George Darby. Eunice loved Old Grannie's stories about Hoofengoofers — the little people who dwell along riverbanks, prairies, and woodlands of the Des Moines River Valley. She especially liked the story of Gergewumpus and the Troll, and dreamed of one day rescuing one of the little men from a trap like the farmer in the tale did. To Eunice these stories was real, and she squirmed in her chair whenever Old Grannie described the nasty troll coming down from Little Switzerland in northeast Iowa to trap Hoofengoofers for its dinner. She loved the part where Gewald Tomnoggins, King of the Hoofengoofers, rewarded the farmer for saving his nephew.

George Darby smiled at this nonsense. He was not interested in Hoofengoofers. What he was interested in was stories of the James Gang and the robberies they committed in southern Iowa. Stories with real value to them. It is a matter of record that Jesse and Frank James did rob some banks in Iowa, and the rumors of other robberies and sightings of the notorious desperados stirred George's blood. This was an interesting reaction for a man whose occupation brought him into regular contact with the likes of Al Capone or the O'Banion Gang. And *they* didn't faze him...

But George's interest was purely practical. It is a known fact — at least according to Old Grannie Linahen — that Cole Younger was wounded by a farmer over by Dexter, and that Frank and Jesse James had to hold up in a nearby woods till he was fit to travel. This was, of course, years before Bonnie Parker and Clyde Barrow visited the same area, much to their discredit. At any rate, the James boys were unable to travel very fast, having to care for the wounded man, and the story goes that they buried the take from their last bank robbery so as to travel lighter. (It is unclear which bank they was supposed to have robbed. Some folks say it was the bank in Pella, while others think it was Luther or Perry.) Now, if only George Darby could find that treasure, why, he could give up hooch running and take life easy.

Early one morning in October, George stopped by Old Grannie Linahen's for breakfast. He'd had a dream the night before, a fateful and portentous dream. He wanted the old lady's advice. In the dream, it had been a moonlit night, and two men were digging a hole behind a large round barn. The men looked like the Smith Brothers on a box of cough drops. They had a large crate full of what looked like bank sacks, and they buried it. Then they got on their horses and rode off into the woods.

Old Grannie Linahen said as how most folks think that the James Gang was Wild West outlaws and looked like cowboys. But in fact, they was more like Missouri hillbillies. Jesse James once had a photographer take a picture of the gang at their cave hideout, and he wore a long, black beard in the photograph just like the Smith Brothers' had. Old Grannie told George that he had dreamed true — of Jesse and Frank James burying the money from the bank robbery at Luther (or Perry... or Pella...). Now if George could find that spot and dig, why, he'd make his fortune, for sure.

Most barns in the Midwest are either square or rectangular. Round barns are rather unique. There were a lot more round barns in Iowa in those days than there are now, but even back then, they were rare. There weren't that many, and George had the advantage of knowing what this one looked like, having seen it in his dream. He took to driving new routes on his hooch runs to Chicago, taking out-of-the-way back roads and asking farmers along the way if they knew of any round barns.

Finally, one day George rushed up Old Grannie Linahen's front porch steps with exciting news. He'd found the round barn at an abandoned farmstead over by Winterset. It was exactly as he had seen it in his dream! Eunice was so excited that he invited her to come along the next night and help dig.

On that crisp autumn night, those two youngsters snuck out to the abandoned farm and began digging behind the old round barn on the spot George had seen in his dream. They found nothing. They dug a little to the east; still nothing. They dug farther down the slope; they dug to the west; and then they went back to the original spot and dug deeper. Nothing. The work was especially hard because they had to fill in the holes afterwards so folks wouldn't know what they were up to.

For two or three nights, George and Eunice labored in vain; but at last, something came of their exertions. In the course of their digging, when they got tired they would sit back against an old cottonwood tree and talk about past disappointments and future hopes; or sometimes they'd just count the stars...

At any rate, it was during one of these occasions when George Darby sudden discovered that he was in love with Eunice Keller. She was not the girl of his dreams by a long shot — her eyes were too big and she had too many freckles — but for many long years afterwards, George always said that he found the real treasure of his life that night.

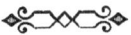

After that, Eunice lost interest in digging for buried treasure. A woman in love has more important things to think about. Like where they would live after they got married, and how many children they might have, and what their names might be...

While she never lost her girlhood sense of wonder, Eunice Keller grew up overnight into a sensible and mature young woman. Like all truly wise women, she also knew that men like her Georgie would never completely grow up. And that was a good thing, for a man without youth becomes jaded and cynical, works himself too hard, and winds up in an early grave. So, understanding, she encouraged George to follow his dream.

Well, sir. George Darby was determined to have money in the bank before they got married. He began making back-to-back hooch runs and took risks with the G-men that he would never have tried in the past. But his faithful old Model-T truck carried him through, and on weekends he would return to the old round barn to dig. Eunice would pack him a midnight picnic basket so he could eat at the farmstead. It was a terrible strain on him, and George took to carrying a gallon crock of Templeton Rye to swig on as he sat there alone under the old cottonwood tree.

It was getting on toward winter, and before long the ground would be frozen hard. But George determined he would keep on digging as long as he could. On a frosty night in November, when he had just finished refilling his last hole, weary to his bone marrow and hardly able to keep his eyes open, George decided he was too tired to drive home. Grabbing some old blankets from his truck, along with the crock of Templeton Rye, he climbed up into the haymow of the old round barn and prepared to sleep in the straw.

Once again, George Darby had a portentous dream. A dream that was to change his life. In the dream, moonlight was streaming down through the high window of the barn, making the motes of straw dust sparkle like faery glamour and casting an strange luminescence on the old board walls, pitchforks, and other barn tools. He dreamed that he was lying on his bed of straw unable to move, and that three *little men* — no taller than rabbits — were engaged in carrying off his crock of Templeton Rye, which he had left on a workbench in the haymow. The crock was for them like a heavy cask, and it took the combined efforts of all three of them to climb down off the bench without dropping it.

Hoofengoofers! *They were Hoofengoofers...*

Dressed like 19th century farmers and wearing floppy wide-brim hats with white owls' feathers in the hat bands. With long beards that dragged down on the floor. Little men. They were exactly like Old Grannie Linahen's stories! *Hoofengoofers!*

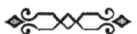

George Darby was not surprised the next morning when he awoke to find that his crock was gone. Nor was he particularly astonished to find tiny bootprints in the dust around the workbench. Tiny footprints. What did surprise him, however, was the gold coin that lay on the bench where he had left his crock. It was like no coin George had ever seen, and he could not read the lettering. It was the size of a silver dollar and three times as thick!

It must be worth over three hundred dollars...

George burned up the main highway driving back to Audubon County. Folks in Templeton remarked seeing him roar into town, and the G-men waved to him as he thundered past their lodgings — but George was long gone before they could get to their cars. George drove to his supplier and spent every last penny he owned on Templeton Rye. The bootlegger gave it to him wholesale at $4.00 a gallon. George then took the most obscure roads and byways back to Madison County, to the farmstead.

He unloaded the entire truckload of Templeton Rye into the old round barn just before nightfall. Then he drove his truck about two miles down the road and waited until the moon come out. He waited another half hour — just for good measure — and then drove back to the old abandoned farmstead.

Every last bottle of Templeton Rye whiskey was gone. And on the barn floor, sitting next to a scrolled parchment, was a sack of gold coins so heavy that George had to back the truck inside the barn and load it with a block-and-tackle. When George and Eunice were married the next weekend, they had enough money in the bank to last them for years. They were able to take life easy, and follow their dreams. George had been wrong when he estimated the value of the gold — each coin was worth over $1200, and the couple shared their good fortune with Old Grannie Linahen. They had lots of Darby children, most of whom are still living.

And to this day, one of the most prized possessions in the family of George and Eunice Darby is the diminutive but ornately calligraphied parchment, found alongside that bag of gold coins, which reads:

Templeton Rye
by special appointment
to His Royal Majesty
GEWALD TOMNOGGINS
King of the Hoofengoofers

Hoofengoofer Hiking Trail

Troll Feathers

Kathryn and Charles Emhoff lived on a nice farmstead in the south part of Story County bordering on the banks of the Skunk River. It was a good farm and provided what in those days was a pretty decent living, though it was a lot of work. The couple had no children and were nearing their forties, but what they lacked in not having youngsters they made up for in the love and companionship they enjoyed with each other. Charlie Emhoff was a hard-working fellow of English descent, a rugged and sturdy man who toiled long hours in his fields. Kate was equally hard working, but was the more imaginative and intelligent of the two. She had been born Katie Moore down in Mt. Ayr, and possessed what the Irish would call the "Gift o' Vision" — which meant that she could see things straight on that most people see only out of the corners of their eyes. Her dreams frequently come to pass, she could call milk from a dry cow, and she was favored by the Little People.

Kate was on friendly terms with a Hoofengoofer named Gump, who lived under an old oak tree in the woods behind their barn on the crest of a bluff overlooking the Skunk River. In the wee hours of the morning, when Kate would get up to milk the cows, Gump would sit on a stump nearby — or perch on the top fence rail — to supervise the milking. Gump was a very old fellow, even for a Hoofengoofer. His beard was three inches longer than he was tall, and he loved to swap tall tales and ancient lore with Kate. Charlie could not to see Gump, but he sometimes heard two voices coming from the barn, and went in to find Kate sitting alone on the milking stool. Other times Charlie would scratch his head in puzzlement over the tiny boot prints he found in the mud behind the dairy barn. Charlie would never admit that he believed in Hoofengoofers, but in his secret heart he knew that Gump was real. Life went on happily on the Emhoff farmstead — until the year of the epidemic when Charlie took sick.

Now Charlie was terrible sick, near on to death, and though Kate nursed him to the best of her ability, she feared she was going to lose the only husband she had ever wanted. The local doctor did what he could, but this was in the days before miracle drugs and there wasn't much you could do but keep the patient in bed, give him herb tea and chicken soup, and try to keep the fever down. The doctor tried different medicines on Charlie, but they didn't help. Kate was desperate.

"What am I going to do, Gump?" she pleaded one morning. "Charlie won't last another week, the way he's going."

"Wal, I ain't much on healin' lore," said the little man, who was sitting on the chicken coup and was no taller than the big red rooster. "But our king — Gewald Tomnoggins — he knows a passle more about everything than I do. He has a healer at his palace named Poltwort, who knows darned near everything. If Old Poltwort can't cure Charlie — then it can't be did."

"Palace?" said Kate. "You Hoofengoofers have a palace? Why, I've never heard of such a thing!"

"Wal, it ain't much of a palace," said Gump. "But us Hoofengoofers like it. 'Tain't like the King of Denmark's place, but it's good enough for us. It's in the woods upriver from here, up between Soaper's Mill and Story City. If ye want, I'll take ye there..."

Kate arranged with her neighbor, Mrs. Anderson, to sit by Charlie until she could return. She was torn between leaving her husband — for fear that he'd die while she wasn't there — and the certainty that he would die otherwise. Kate and Gump set off upriver, stopping by the little man's house first so he could lock up.

There was a tiny door set into the exposed roots on the downhill side of the big oak tree, and Gump scurried inside while Kate peeked in through a little window. Within the Hoofengoofer's home, she could see a cozy miniature parlour furnished with 19th century chairs, tables, and cupboards arranged around a hearthrug and little fireplace. Gump fetched his overcoat and hiking stick, and returned presently, locking his little door behind him.

Now all this happened long before the county established the Green Belt area along the Skunk River south of Story City. The woods was thicker back then, but Kate and Gump made good time. They come to what Kate at first thought was a logjam of driftwood and branches from the summer floods — but on looking closer, she saw what no human without the Gift o' Vision could have seen.

The pile of branches and driftwood was in actuality a tiny lodge, with gables and turrets, and looked for all the world like a miniature stave church like the ones you see in Scandinavia. On the grassy bank around it was Hoofengoofers: some grooming woodchucks, others herding rabbits, little children playing Hoofengames...

Kate waited nearby while Gump went into the woodland palace to speak to his king. He returned twenty minutes later with Gewald Tomnoggins himself, Old Poltwort the healer, and twenty or forty other Hoofengoofers, who were merely curious. Kate was delighted to see so many of the Little People in one place, but it was the King of the Hoofengoofers who commend her attention most.

Gewald Tomnoggins said to Kate Emhoff, "Gump has told us many good things about your man Charlie. We are sad to hear of his illness, but we have for you a glimmer of hope. Poltwort the healer can make a poultice of herbs, mushrooms, and mud — and one other ingredient — that can heal any illness and break any fever."

"Oh, please, if you would only help..." said Kate, but the king held up his hand.

"There is one problem," he said. "My people can gather all but the last ingredient from the woodlands around here. But that final thing — the most important part — is something no Hoofengoofer would ever willingly go to fetch, and I cannot command them to do so."

"What is this other ingredient?" asked Kate. "I'll get it myself if I can. What is it?"

The King of the Hoofengoofers looked at her with a solemn expression on his face and said, "troll feathers."

Then, seeing the expression on Kate's face, Gewald Tomnoggins added, "To give the medicine its power, the poultice must have three freshly plucked feathers ... from a troll."

Now Kate Emhoff had never heard of a troll having feathers. Feathered trolls are rare, even in Norway where trolls originally come from. Not one troll in ten-thousand is born with feathers, and since there are less than ten-thousand trolls in all America, finding a troll with feathers in Iowa is pretty darned rare indeed.

"But you're not out-of-luck," piped in Old Poltwort. "There used to be a Feather Troll up near Decorah by the name of Rastover. There's lots of trolls up in that area around the Ice Cave. My grandmother had one of Rastover's feathers when I was a little hoof. Mebee you can get some from him."

"Fat chance," grumbled Gump. "Rastover was the nastiest of all the bad-tempered trolls. He'd never do favors for nobody."

"Well, if it's troll feathers I need to save Charlie, it's troll feathers I'll get," said Kate, "if I have to pick old Rastover up by his ears and shake him till his teeth rattle."

"I'll bet you get them, too," said Gewald Tomnoggins. "And while you're in troll country, I have a favor I'd ask of you."

"Anything," said Kate.

"Many years ago, my daughter Lina was lost in the woods," said the king. "We found a piece of her frock in the teeth of a troll's trap. There's little hope of her being alive if she was carried off to be a troll's dinner. But if I could only know for certain, I'd sleep better at night."

"I'll do what I can," said Kate.

Kate Emhoff sent word to Mrs. Anderson that she'd be gone for several days to fetch medicine. There was summer flooding in northern Iowa that year, and Kate had to detour far to the south and east. The Cedar, Wapsipinicon, and Turkey Rivers were all impassable, so Kate hitched a wagon ride to the German colonies at Amana. She arrived after most of the folks was in bed, and spent the night with a kindly wine merchant whose winery was the only building in town with a light showing.

At breakfast the next morning, she learned that the winemaker had a dilemma. "The floods drowned my grape vines this spring," he told her. "Even the orchards are blighted, so I can't even make apple wine. If you find these magic trollfeathers you're seeking, bring me one for luck. I'll certainly need all the luck I can get to survive next winter."

"I'll do what I can," said Kate.

"And take care if you find trolls," said the wine merchant with a chuckle. "I hear they are spiteful, tricky little creatures."

Kate made her way northeast to Dubuque, where she spent the night with the nuns at a nearby convent. Even the holy sisters had their difficulties. Kate learned that they'd had trouble with food spoiling, milk going sour, accidental breakage of valuable items, and even money gone missing. "Now, who would steal money from nuns," Kate wondered to herself.

The sisters were disconcerted when they heard Kate's mission. "Rastover is a vicious and violent troll," said the mother superior. "Now not all trolls are nasty — but you watch out for the ones that are. Rastover is the worst. He's mean because his feathers itch."

When Kate was nearly asleep that night, the youngest nun in the convent come quietly to her bedside and whispered in her ear. "Mother Superior might not approve of me telling you this," she said. "But I grew up in Decorah and I know about trolls. There is a hidden cliff with seven caves. Most people don't know about it. The seventh cave — the one on the north — is Rastover's lair. You must never go there at night. Only go midday, when Rastover is out hunting or stealing lutefisk. Rastover is a terrible monster and he'll kill you if he catches you in his cave. But during the day his wife is there, and she might help you — she's as kind and friendly as Rastover is evil."

Kate whispered, "Thank you."

The youngest nun blushed and added, "If you find trollfeathers, bring me one as a sign from God that our luck has changed."

"I'll do what I can," said Kate.

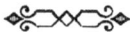

The next day, Kate came at last to Decorah, Iowa. Because this was in the early autumn, there was still several hours of daylight left before nightfall. Kate followed the directions given her by the youngest nun, and found the Cliff of Seven Caves. The cliff was steep and rocky. The first three caves on the south were halfway down the cliff and fairly large. The fourth cave was higher and somewhat smaller, its entrance grown over with weeds and brambles. The next two caves were far to the north and quite small. The last cave stood alone at the farthest end, where the cliff was steepest, the rocks sharpest, and the handholds few and far between. To reach Rastover's den, Kate had to climb down to the first cave and then make her way from cave to cave along the cliff face. It was a difficult climb.

Kate Emhoff made her way finally to the last cave. It was empty. But at the back, behind a large rock, she found a crack that led into a smaller and much smellier cave. It was also empty. But at the back of it was a small oak door on rusty iron hinges with an iron ring for a handle. Since it was daytime and Rastover was probably gone, Kate knocked on the little wooden door, hoping the troll's wife was as kind and friendly as the youngest nun had said she was. A tiny golden voice from within said, "Please enter." Kate pulled open the door and crawled into the smallest cave yet. The smell was horrid.

Rastover's den was cluttered with all manner of junk. An old open-wire coil-spring mattress covered with straw and weeds was laid across two large logs to make a bed. A wooden cable-spool turned endwise made a dining table. Piles of bones and filth had been tossed into a corner. Objects stolen from dustbins and junkyards decorated the lair. There was a moose skull mounted on the wall, a brass spittoon full of dead cockroaches at the bedside (for snacks), a box full of half-eaten cigars on an old packing crate, a heavy wicker bird cage containing a large toy doll, a wind-up phonograph stacked high with cow patties, and the pelts and hides of previously devoured skunks, snakes, vultures, and weasels. And over everything brooded the noisome, horrid, nauseating odor of lutefisk!

It is a known fact that trolls came over from Norway on ships full of immigrants. A few were even said to have come with Leif Erickson and his Vikings. But the only trolls that persist today are the ones that found cool caves where they could survive the summer heat and which are near to Norwegian settlements where they can steal lutefisk. There is said to be some vital element in lutefisk which is essential to trolls' health. Rastover was an exceptionally healthy troll.

The small golden voice spoke from the bird cage. It was not a doll after all! It was a tiny, beautiful girl with long flaxen curls. "Who are you?" she said. "What are you doing here, it's very dangerous!"

"Are you the troll's wife?" asked Kate. When the beautiful girl nodded, she went on to explain. "My name is Kate Emhoff. My husband is dying and you must help me save his life."

After Kate had told her story, the troll's wife said, "I will help you, but in return you must take me with you when you leave. I am a prisoner here. Rastover keeps me locked in this cage whenever he goes out. He'll be home soon. You must hide under the bed tonight. It will be most dangerous when he first comes home if he smells you. But after eating his dinner, the smell of lutefisk will mask your presence. Rastover always gets sleepy on a full stomach, and after that you'll be safe.

And so it happened. Kate crawled underneath the low bed. When Rastover come home with a bagful of carrion and roadkill, he sniffed the air and started to say *fee, fie, foe, fum*, but his wife interrupted and said, "Oh, shut up and let me out of this cage so I can fix your supper."

Rastover was huge for an Iowa troll — as big as a turkey — and he was covered with brilliant, autumn-colored plumage: rusty-brown feathers with white tips, jet black plumes, bright red quills, and speckled down. Rastover's nose was like a huge potato with bumps and starting to sprout. His eyes were like tiny black rocks with red centers. His lips were thick and flabby, with fangs three or four inches long. Rastover was as ugly as his feathers were beautiful. He ate for his dinner that night three dead skunks (one of which was particularly ripe), six rotted crow carcasses, and three barrels of lutefisk — which he washed down with warm beer and turpentine. After that, he belched deeply and crawled onto his bed with his wife. Soon he was snoring. The troll's wife waited a full hour to make certain that Rastover was asleep. Then the tiny girl reached over and pulled out one of Rastover's plume feathers with a pop.

"OWwwwrr!" roared the troll as he awoke and sat up in his bed (nearly squashing Kate, who was still hiding underneath). "Ye've pulled out one of me feathers, wife! Wot are ye thinking of?"

"Oh, husband, dear! I was having a nightmare. I dreamed of a convent where food spoiled, milk went sour, valuables were smashed, and money's gone missing."

"Wife, that were no nightmare," said Rastover. "You've been dreaming true. There's a convent in Dubuque what's being plagued by a Jinxmeister. If only they knew, the nuns could be rid of it in an instant by making fine caramels. Jinxmeisters love mischief and discord, and they hate sweet things. Caramels would drive it away screaming. It's rather funny. Now let me get back to sleep."

The troll's wife waited another hour to make certain that her husband was soundly asleep again. Then she reached over and pulled out another of the troll's fine plume feathers. "OWwwwrr!!" roared Rastover as he awoke and sat up. "Ye've pulled out another of me feathers! Wot are ye thinking of, wife?"

"Oh, husband, dear! I was having a nightmare again. I dreamed of a winery where the master can make no wine because his orchards and vineyards are ruined."

"Wife, that were no nightmare," said Rastover. "You've been dreaming true. That wine merchant could make all the wine he needed from a common plant that grows abundantly on every farmstead in Iowa, if only he knew. Rhubarb wine is finer than anything made from grapes, apples, or any other fruit. That wine merchant is just a fool. Now let me get back to sleep."

The troll's wife waited yet another hour till her husband was soundly asleep and snoring. Then she reached over and pulled out a third of the troll's fine plume feathers. "OWwwwrr!!" roared Rastover as he awoke and sat up. "Ye've pulled out yet another of me fine feathers! Wot are ye thinking of, wife?"

"Oh, husband, dear! I was having another nightmare. This time I dreamed of a woodland palace where a king mourns for his lost daughter."

"Wife, that were no nightmare," said Rastover. "You've been dreaming true. Ye've been dreaming of yer own home and yer dear sweet father, neither of which ye've seen since the day I caught ye in that trap for me supper. But Princess, ye were so lovely that I couldn't bear to eat ye, so I brought ye home to be me wife. But ye'll never see yer woodland home again, except in dreams. Now let me get back to sleep."

Next morning, Rastover locked his wife up in the wicker cage, hung the key on the moose antlers, took up his bag, and set off hunting. Quicker than a dragonfly, Kate scrambled out from under the bed, grabbed the key, and set the princess free — for it was indeed Liralina Tomnoggins, Princess of the Hoofengoofers!

They waited until Rastover was well away and then set out for home with the three troll feathers. They stayed with the nuns in Dubuque that night and told them what Rastover had said about the Jinxmeister. The holy sisters began cooking the finest caramels in the world, and do so to this very day. Their luck changed overnight, and the Jinxmeister ran screaming in agony.

Kate and Lina spent the next night with the wine merchant in the Amana Colonies, and piestengle — rhubarb wine — has been brewed there ever since, much to the wine merchant's profit.

Princess Liralina was tearfully reunited with Gewald Tomnoggins, King of the Hoofengoofers. Poltwort the healer made a poultice of herbs, mushrooms, mud, and three feathers freshly plucked from a troll — and Charlie Emhoff recovered fully. Everyone would have lived happily ever after, except...

When Rastover the Troll returned to his cave, he was furious to find that his wife had escaped. He roared and raged and vowed revenge. He swore to find whoever had "stolen" his wife and kill the thief and her whole family and anyone else who had helped them. He stomped and spit and scurried out of his cave with his nose to the ground to follow their scent. With his great nose, Rastover could follow anyone anywhere. He made his way down from the highlands and into the prairies, hot on the trail.

Unfortunately for Rastover, it was pheasant season.

On the wall of a small town tavern in northeast Iowa he is stuffed and mounted above the bar, with a bronze plaque which reads:

Biggest Dang Pheasant Ever Shot in Iowa

PART TWO

The Englishman Who Wanted to Be a Sourdough and Other Alaskan Stories

The Englishman Who Wanted to Be a Sourdough

Based on a poem by Robert Service

This here's the story of the Englishman who wanted to be a sourdough. Now the glaciers along the St. Elias Mountains are said to be inhabited by giant white worms, a story that probably originated with the Southern Tutchone tribe legends. Ordinary ice worms range in size from one to three centimeters long and are white, yellow, brown, or black in color. But the giant ice worms of the St. Elias Mountains are bluish-white, with bright red eyes. In the days of the Gold Rush up in the Yukon Territory, Ice Worm Cocktails was said to be popular among the sourdoughs and prospectors that panned for gold along the Dawson Trail.

Well, sir. One day there come to Dawson a feller that was as unlike anything them prospectors had ever seen before in their lives. Percy Brown was his name, and he come from London-on-the-Thames. And this feller had a monocle in his eye and knee-stockings on his legs. On the shoulder of his coat, he had a leather pad to rest his gun on. It seems that Major Percy Brown fancied hisself a great hunter. A big game hunter. Why, he'd hunted kangaroos in the Murrumbidgee wilds and shot cassowary on the plains of Timbuktu. Now, he'd come to the Klondike to hunt Arctic fox and white hare, mebbe even shoot hisself a bear or two and perchance bag a moose.

Yessir, Major Percy Brown was an Englishman right down to his skin and bones, and he stuck out like a sore thumb among them grizzled prospectors and sourdough fellers. Why, when he come to Dawson, Major Brown acted like he owned the place, and was shootin' off his mouth a good deal more than he ever shot his gun. Finally, the boys just couldn't take it no more. One day, Skipper Gray and Deacon White was sittin' in their shack sippin' on a jug of whiskey along with Sheriff Black.

And Skipper Gray sez, "You know, this English feller, Major Brown — why, he's sticking out his chest as if he owned the whole town of Dawson.

The Sheriff sez, "He called hisself a sourdough when he'd only been here a week."

And the Deacon sez, "You know, boys — I have a plan by which we can test this feller and see what he's really made of. Meet me at the Malamute Saloon tonight, and we'll turn this Piccadilly Dude into a real sourdough.

Well, that night, a bunch of the boys was whooping' it up at the Malamute Saloon. The fun was fast and furious, and the hooch was a-flowin'. There was a feller ticklin' the ivories and a couple of dancing gals up on the stage. Some of them old prospectors was gettin' so excited they was shootin' off their guns into the ceiling. They was all roarin' and hootin' and carryin' on like anything. And then, right into the eye of the hurricane, walked Major Percy Brown.

The gallant Major Brown, like an apparition, with his monocle in his eye — an' he was wearin' "plus-fours" knickers. And he had knee-stockings up to here. And he had that fancy hunting jacket with the leather on the shoulder for when he was carryin' his rifle. And he had one of them tweed deer-stalker caps with the two visors and ear flaps tied up over the top of his head. I tell you, he was a dandy.

Now when all them prospectors saw Percy standin' there, they began cheerin' like anything. There were shouts of stark amazement and whoops of sheer delight. They all gathered 'round him and slapped him on the back and shook his hand.

Then the Deacon went up to him and said, "Welcome — welcome to the Great White North!"

Well, sir. Percy Brown was blushin' like a young girl. And the Deacon sez, "You know, we are honored to have a man of your stature in our community. Now the boys have talked it over, and they have decided that they would like to initiate you — we would like to make you a *bona fide* sourdough. Now some folks say that you ain't a sourdough till you seen the Yukon ice go out in the springtime. And there's others that say you ain't a real sourdough till you've taken a pick and shovel and worked a claim that you dug out with your own hands. But the most profound authorities on the subject are all agreed that you ain't a sourdough till you've drunk down an Ice Worm Cocktail."

"Well, by Gad!" said Major Brown. "That's ripping, don't you know! I've always wanted to be a certified sourdough. Now while I am certain that your winter ice must be pretty spectacular when it goes out, I'm afraid that I may not still be here for the breakup of your icepack. By Jove! I hope you will excuse my ignorance; I know what a cocktail is — but just what exactly is an ice worm? I never heard of such a thing!"

Deacon White sez, "Well, don't let that bother you none. 'Taint surprisin' that you never heard of 'em, because ice worms is peculiar to the Mountain of Blue Snow up north of here. Most folks outside the Yukon never heard of 'em. You see, way off to the north, up in the Arctic Circle beyond the polar rim, there's a great, solitary peak of ice — it's a marvelous spectacle! — and when the sun shines down from the bright blue sky onto that great mass of glacial ice, it's like a huge jewel sparklin' and glistenin' like a diamond. The sight of it thrills you thru and thru. The pinnacle of this mountain of ice is white as snow, but the base of it is blue as a sapphire. And the ice is just as clear as glass.

"And when you get up close, you can see peering out at you — thousands and thousands of them great ice worms! Now, they're not these tiny little ice worms like they got around here, no sir.

Some of these critters are as big as four or five inches long, and because there's no food for them there in this mountain of ice, no other source of nourishment — why, the only thing there is there for them to eat *is each other's tails.*

"Now of course, the little ice worms don't last very long — they get et up by the bigger ones. Then when the ice and snow melt in the springtime, and the tundra begins to turn green — why, then the ice worms begin to burrow down deep into the ground, and they are not seen again until the following winter."

"I say — that's quite a remarkable yarn," said Major Brown. "But I guess if I'm going to swallow a cocktail with one of these worms in it, you know, I'd like to see one of the little beasts first."

"Well, that ain't no problem," said the Deacon. "Bartender — go bring us some of them pickled ice worms that you got left over from last season."

"Wal, ah dunno," said Bill the bartender. "There's been quite a run on ice worm cocktails, boss. Ah don't think ah got a single ice worm left. Oh, wait a minute! By Golly, there's some extra big ones that we pickled and put away to show to them scientists from down in the States. Lemme see if ah can find 'em. Ah think ah got 'em here in a drawer."

Well, sir. Bill the bartender rummaged around in his drawer, and finally he found a jar — which he brought out with due respect and proper pride, and he set it carefully on the bar. And inside the jar, spiraled in queasy rings or coiled into little balls, there was mebbe a couple dozen gray, greasy things all drowned in alcohol. Their bellies was a bilious bluish-white color, and their eyes was bright red.

Then with great gusto and a fork, the bartender speared one of 'em. It must have been over four inches long, from the tip of its tail to its snout, and the Deacon cried in delight, he sez: "Say — ain't that one a beaut?"

Major Percy Brown sniffed. "I think it's most disgusting. The sight of it gives me the pip. Oh, you chaps are just spoofin' me. You'll never swallow one of those things."

"The hell I won't," said the Deacon. "Hey, Bill — this one's just fine. Fix up four Ice Worm Cocktails, and just pop that big feller into mine."

So Bill the bartender got busy — and with the air of an artist, he began to prepare the Ice Worm Cocktails. He got out four crystal glasses that sparkled and gleamed in the lamplight. Then he set them out there in a shining row. And into each glass he poured two shots of Red Eye Whiskey and a shot of Everclear. And then right down into the middle of each glass he plunked one of them big, fat, juicy ice worms. Some of them suckers was a full six inches long. While the bartender was mixin' the drinks, a hush fell over the Malamute Saloon, and all of them old prospectors gathered 'round close to watch.

"AHHH — that looks *fine!*" said the Deacon, holding his cocktail glass up to the light so he could see the ice worm floating around inside. And Skipper Gray and the Sheriff each lifted their glasses up high. The crowd got tense and quiet.

"Drink up, stranger!" said the Deacon. "Drink up, and you'll be one of us. You'll be a real *sourdough!*"

"Y-you can't bluff me," said the Major. "You'll never drink that ghastly thing."

But then, as the Englishman watched in astonishment, the Deacon and the Skipper and the Sheriff each raised up their glasses and drained their Ice Worm Cocktails in one swallow, and then set their glasses down on the bar with a thump.

With a woebegone look on his face, the Major peered into his own glass — and it seemed that the little ice worm inside was leering out at him. Every eye in the room was on the Major. No one spoke. A hushed expectation filled the waiting, watching crowd. The Major's hand fumbled. Then the Englishman reached out for his glass, and the sourdoughs began to cheer. But then his hand faltered and he drew it back. A few of the boys made rude remarks about him. Finally, gathering all of his nerve, Percy gripped his gleaming glass and raised it to his lips. He tried to take a little sip, but out of the depths of his glass, the little ice worm seemed to raise its head and look at him, and its eyes was bright, ruby red.

And then one of the miners sez, "This dandy-pansy comes in here and struts around like he owns the place. Come on, show us your guts!"

And the mob roared: "Come on, Major! *Prove* to us that you're a sourdough. Drink your cocktail down!"

The Major took another look in his glass, then closed his eyes. Then he raised it to his mouth. But even with his eyes closed, in his mind Percy could see that nasty little worm wiggling around in his drink. The crowd of miners and prospectors gathered 'round him in a ring. And they gloated and they taunted him. Finally, gathering every ounce of his strength, every atom of his will power, Percy choked, gulped, and swallowed down his Ice Worm Cocktail.

The crowd cried in a roar: "Hooray, hooray for Sourdough Brown." With shouts, they raised him up on their shoulders and gave a rousing cheer. But though they praised him to the sky, the Major did not hear them. Amid their gleeful cheering and delight, Percy looked rather sick. A clammy sweat was on his brow, and he was pale as a sheet.

"I... I feel I must be going now," he said plaintively.

"Oh, no!" they said. "Hey — stay and have some more drinks, have a few smokes, and a mebbe a nice big meal..."

But Percy, with a sudden bolt, ran for the door and made his getaway. No one in Dawson has seen him since. But the story is still told in the Yukon to this day, of the night when Major Percy Brown of London drank an Ice Worm Cocktail with a worm in it — that was really just a piece of spaghetti colored with blue food coloring and two red spots on it for eyes.

Si Tanner's Eskimo Parka

This here's the story of Si Tanner's Eskimo Parka. Now my Grandpa Brewer was twenty-one years of age when gold was discovered in the Klondike. So, of course, he set off for the Great White North to seek his fortune. When he come to Skagway, Alaska, there was thousands of prospectors all headed for the Yukon Territory across the border in Canada.

Most of them prospectors traveled the Chilkoot Trail and crossed the Chilkoot Pass on foot. Others hiked up to the White Pass and on into the Yukon Territory, where they proceeded to the headwaters of the Yukon River. There, some thirty grueling miles from where they'd landed, them prospectors built rafts and boats that would take 'em the final *five hundred miles* down the Yukon River to Whitehorse an' Dawson City, near the gold fields.

Them stampeders was met at the international border by the Royal Canadian Mounted Police. To be allowed to enter Canada, they had to carry with 'em a year's supply of goods when they crossed over the passes, which was about a ton of food. And when — or if — they finally got to the gold fields, most of the good claims was already filed. Only a hundred and sixty fellers actually made it up to the Klondike out of over 1,600 that started out from Skagway.

Grandpa Brewer realized that the odd of striking it rich with a gold mine was slimmer than a starving coyote during a famine, and he also figgered out that the folks who was *really* making money was them that sold liquor *and* women to the prospectors and the folks that ran the steamships that brought the gold hunters up to Skagway and carried the gold back down to the States.

Grandpa always said it was the steamship companies who really struck it rich during the Gold Rush. Accordingly, Grandpa Brewer got hisself a job with the Walston Packet Steamship Line as a clerk to the company agent, who had a little shack office down near the wharf.

Now in them days, Skagway was a wide-open town, with saloons and gamblin' houses and loose women and liquor on every block. It was no place for a good Presbyterian like Grandpa —and he did not remain one for very long.

In the days before statehood, Alaska was a military district so they had a barracks and some soldiers and such-like there in Skagway. There was also a U.S. marshal's office, with a man by the name of Sylvester S. Taylor as the marshal. He was crooked as a dog's hind leg.

The real authority in Skagway was a grifter by the name of Soapy Smith. He was known as King of the Frontier Confidence Men. As a crime boss, Soapy ran a large and forceful gang of talented swindlers and rogues. Soapy was known in newspapers around the nation as the Uncrowned King of Skagway. His motto was "Get it while the gettin' is good." Soapy was known for his generosity to the poor and his loyalty to his gang. In them days of the Klondike Gold Rush, no one proved hisself to be more slippery than ol' Soapy Smith.

Well, sir. On the day in question, Marshal Sylvester Taylor was down in Haines, Alaska, which was mebbe thirteen miles down the Taiya Inlet from Skagway, jes' beyond where the Lutak Inlet branched off to the west. Back in Skagway, Soapy Smith and his boys was runnin' a rip-roaring game of Three Card Monte over at Horse-Hair Sadie's Saloon, fleecin' a bunch of sourdoughs out of the gold dust they'd jes' brought down from Canada. The saloon was run by Horse-Hair Sadie herself, the toughest old gal in the North. Sadie was watchin' the game an' feedin' her big ol' fat tomcat poppy seeds, which the critter seemed to think was a rare delicacy. Down at the wharf, Grandpa Brewer and the Walston-Packet agent (a feller by the name of Homer Finche) was supervisin' the loading of a shipment of gold down to Juneau, Alaska, aboard the steamship *Chilkoot Belle*.

Now the Walston Packet Steamship Line owned two small but swift steamers called the *Chilkoot Belle* and the *Chilkoot Queen*. They was sister ships, alike as two peas in a pod, except that the *Belle* had a bright yellow pilot house and a green funnel, while the *Queen's* pilot house was a fine blue color an' she had a red smokestack. The two ships worked at opposite ends of the Inside Passage between Skagway and Juneau. The *Queen* would take on supplies an' passengers (would-be prospectors, that is) down at Juneau, whilst the *Belle* would load up with gold nuggets and bags of gold dust up in Skagway. Then the *Queen* would start north and the *Belle* would head south; it took about a day for the run each way. The two ships would usually meet about mid-way along the Lynn Canal, and they'd exchange blasts on their steam-whistles by way of greetings. When they got to where they was headed, they'd unload and take on new cargo and passengers for their return trips, and then whistle at each other again when they met on the way back.

Now you may be wonderin' what all this has to do with Si Tanner's Eskimo Parka. Well, jes' hold onto your britches — I'm comin' to that.

This story begins on January 13, 1898, in the middle of the cold Alaskan winter. It seems on that particular day, the Hayes Bonanza Mine up in Whitehorse had recently struck it rich. They was sendin' the biggest cargo o' gold ever shipped south to the States. Grandpa Brewer and Homer Finche was supervisin' the boys they'd hired to load up the Hayes Bonanza shipment, checkin' the cargo off against the manifests and bills o' lading, or whatever you call them. Once the *Belle* was under steam and headed south for Juneau, there warn't much else for Grandpa to do till the *Queen* arrived the next day. So Grandpa jes' sat on a bench and whittled on a model of the *Chilkoot Belle* that he was a-carvin'.

The problem was that when the *Queen* finally did arrive an' the passengers was gettin' off the ship, the captain told Homer Finche that they hadn't seen the *Belle* on their way up the Passage. Now with a shipment of gold the size of what the *Belle* had been a-carryin', this threw Homer Finche into a frenzy. The officers at the army barracks said that the *Belle* was a civilian ship, so it warn't none of their business what happened to her; and the deputy marshal was dumb as a brick and wouldn't help. So straightaway, Homer Finche hired Josias M. Tanner to investigate the mystery of the disappeared steamship. (Tanner was better known to his pals as "Si" Tanner.) Captain Tanner ran his own small steamship and a string of barges, horses, and wagons. which he used to transfer goods from ship to shore. He had been appointed a member of the Law and Order Committee by Skagway's city council in November 1897.

Now Captain Si Tanner had the reputation of being the straightest man in Alaska. He was stalwart and strong and clever, a good tracker and honest as the day is long. He always wore his favorite Eskimo parka, which he'd had custom made for him by a tribe of Inuits up north of Fairbanks. This was the finest parka in the Great White North — it had the most beadwork and the finest white wolf fur, and the leather was all lined with fluffy sheepskin that he'd had sent up from the States. Si Tanner was more proud of his parka than anything else in the world.

Captain Tanner was a big man, strong but kinda laid back most of the time. When he'd be a-talkin' to you, he'd lean back against the wall with one foot tucked up behind him and one of his big hands restin' casually on his knee. But then when he got riled, Si Tanner went into action — and nobody in Skagway cared to go up against him.

Si Tanner and Homer Finche talked to the captain and the pilot of the *Chilkoot Queen* — but there warn't no help there.

The pilot said the *Queen* shoulda passed the *Belle* long before dark the previous day.

Well, sir. Finche chartered a steam launch and the two men headed south to look for the *Chilkoot Belle* and to fetch Marshall Taylor back from Haines. The steamship agent left Grandpa Brewer in charge of the office there in Skagway.

Grandpa hung around the *Chilkoot Queen* — it being the only company business in town at the time. The *Queen* had brought up a load of salt pork destined for Whitehorse, and the crew was waiting for the agents who'd ordered it to come pick up their shipment. There was fifty barrels of meat in the hold, so Grandpa Brewer busied hisself checking the manifest against the order that had been placed with Homer Finche three weeks before.

The steam launch was a swift little craft; she could run up to six miles an hour with a good head of steam. So it was only mid-afternoon when Si Tanner and Homer Finche returned from Haines with the marshal. There had been no sign of the *Chilkoot Belle* along the way, and there was no tributaries or side branches north of Taiyasanka Harbor where she might have been waylaid. Marshal Taylor said that he had not seen the *Belle* the day before, which he thought was odd because the ship usually stopped at Haines to take on mail. He said he did see the *Queen* on her way north. The marshal thought the *Belle* must have sunk somewheres along the thirteen-mile stretch between Haines and Skagway — but Si Tanner said there was no sign of any such shipwreck.

Homer Finche posted a reward of $1000 in cash for finding the *Chilkoot Belle,* and another $500 for recovery of the gold. He and Si Tanner mustered up a group of volunteers and spent far into the night carefully searching every inch of the banks on both sides of the waterway all the way to Haines. Grandpa Brewer was left behind at the Skagway shipping office to act as liaison or something such-like.

When the searchers returned about 3:00 a.m. the next morning, covered with snow, hungry and half-frozen, Homer Finche and Si Tanner stomped into the steamship office and knocked the ice off their mukluks. Grandpa Brewer had a roarin' fire burning in the iron woodstove, with some glasses and a bottle of whisky ready and waiting. Si Tanner hung his great parka up on a nail, took off his wet fur mittens, grabbed a glass of whisky, and huddled down next to a shivvering Homer Finche before the fire.

Grandpa walked over and examined the backside of Si Tanner's Eskimo parka, chewed his lower lip, and nodded wisely.

"What yew lookin' at, boy?" said Si Tanner, and the big man strode over to look at his coat. "Well, damn!" he shouted. "The dang thing is ruined! It's all stained to hell on the back."

Grandpa waited till the feller got finished yellin' and swearin', and then he said: "You know, sir, if you want to find out who did this to your coat, get it back on and come with me. You, too, boss." Grandpa then lit a kerosene lamp and headed out the door.

Homer Finche and Si Tanner reluctantly got their winter gear back on and followed Grandpa out of the office and down to the wharf where the *Chilkoot Queen* was moored. The big steamer was dark and silent; there warn't a crewman in sight. Grandpa Brewer led the two older men down into the hold where the fifty barrels of salt pork was stored.

Grandpa said: "The crew woulda taken this stuff off tonight — but I sent 'em a little present first. I gave 'em three bottles of Sadie's Hairball Brandy."

"What?" roared Homer Finche. "Them boys won't be fit to work for three days! That stuff will make you see the Northern Lights on a pitch-black night!"

In reply, Grandpa jes' pried the lid off one of them kegs of salt pork and removed several hunks of preserved meat. There, beneath the chunks of briny pork — glitterin' in the kerosene lamplight — was gold.

Every barrel in the hold of the *Chilkoot Queen* was full of gold.

Well, then, you jes' shoulda seen ol' Si Tanner go into action. He had them drunken crewmen and fake officers up against the wall before they knew what had hit them. Of course, it warn't the *Chilkoot Queen* a-tall — it was the *Chilkoot Belle,* with her pilot house and smokestack repainted. It all come out the next day, after the fake captain and crew was in irons and the real crew was rescued from the storeroom in which they was locked.

It seems that the morning before, about eight miles below Skagway, the captain and pilot of the *Chilkoot Belle* had spied a bunch of empty barrels floating in the water ahead, blocking the passage. A bunch of rough-lookin' men with rifles and pistols stood in a flatboat to one side. The captain was about to order the steamship to ram the blockage when he felt the barrel of a gun pressed against the back of his neck. Some of the hijackers had been passengers on the southbound run of the *Chilkoot Belle.*

The real crew was locked in the storage room, an' the empty barrels was brought aboard and loaded with gold and salt pork from the flat boat. The fake captain and pilot was men the hijackers had hired down in Seattle. The pilot house and funnel was repainted. They changed the name on the sides, and the ship simply turned around and steamed right back up to Skagway. The real *Chilkoot Queen* was still down in Juneau with engines that had been sabotaged by the hijackers so the ship couldn't show up and spoil their game. It took nearly two weeks before her engines was fixed.

Well, sir. Marshal Taylor said that he must have been mistaken when he thought he saw the *Queen* northbound on the waterway. But most folks thought he was in on the deal with the hijackers. They could never prove it, though, and it was later that year before Marshal Taylor was arrested for another crime and Si Tanner took over as U.S. marshal in Skagway. He later went on to become a senator for the Territory of Alaska.

Folks always figgured it was Soapy Smith who had planned the whole thing, but they couldn't pin it on him. He was slippery as soap. While the hijacking was going on, Soapy was hot in the middle of a poker game over at Horse-Hair Sadie's Saloon, with plenty of witnesses to his whereabouts. None of the hijackers ever talked about who was their boss that had organized the whole operation. Soapy's gang was always real loyal to him.

Six months later, during Skagway's first Fourth of July celebration, Soapy Smith was grand marshal of the parade, sittin' right alongside of Alaskan Territorial Governor John Brady. Yes, sir. That was jes' four days before Soapy met up with a band of vigilantes. Soapy Smith's last words was, "My God, don't shoot!"

Of course, Grandpa Brewer had figured out the whole mystery before the search party had even set out — when he'd seen that yellow paint on the back of Si Tanner's Eskimo parka. The big man had leaned against the pilot house when he was a-talkin' to the fake captain and the pilot on the morning of the hijacking. The paint wasn't completely dry yet. That was the clue that let Grandpa solve the crime. He'd had to wait until after dark to check out his deductions, after those bottles of Hairball Brandy had made certain the lookouts that was guardin' the gold wouldn't catch Grandpa sneakin' into the hold of the steamship.

So Grandpa Brewer got the $1,500 reward, which he was offered in cash. But Grandpa said he'd rather have it in the form of stock in the Walston Packet Steamship Line. Grandpa always said it was the steamship companies who really struck it rich during the Gold Rush. By the time he was twenty-eight years old, Grandpa Brewer was chairman of the board.

Kaintuck and the Frenchman

Now long before th' Louisiana Purchase, New Orleans was under the jurisdiction of France or Spain. (The two kings would use the Louisiana Territory to wager on during their card games, so it switched back and forth from French to Spanish rule fairly often).

Both the French and the Spanish was big on honour and etiquette and all kinds of nobility hogwash. They would challenge each other to duels at th' drop of a hat. There was two gigantic old live oak trees in New Orleans back during them days that the duels would take place under.

It were quite a festive event when two of them fellers would decide to shoot it out or stab at each other with swords. Fancy ladies with gowns an' parasols escorted by aristocratic dudes with high hats an' canes would turn out at the Dueling Oaks at th' crack of dawn to watch, and there was all kinds of rules and etiquettes.

The feller who was challenged allas got to pick th' weapon and the place where th' duel was to happen. O' course, they near to always picked the Dueling Oaks, and the weapons was either swords or else them fancy-pants silver dueling pistols with engraved filigree.

Well, sir. All was fine and dandy until the Louisiana Purchase transferred New Orleans over to the USA.

With a new place ripe for prosperity, there soon come hordes of carpetbaggers from up north and Kaintuck hillbillies from the mountains. The latter would come down the Mississippi

River on log rafts to sell their wares, and many of 'em would stay on 'cause they liked New Orleans.

Of course, them hillbillies knew nothin' about the etiquette of dueling. When they fought, it was usually in a tavern or back alley, an' they was roaring drunk. They didn't use swords or fancy dueling pistols — they used bowie knives, bludgeons, double-barreled shotguns, or their own massive fists.

It weren't long before the Kaintucks offended the sensibilities of highbrow Frenchman and Spaniards an' got challenged to duels. But the aristocratic noblemen didn't quite know what to do when the man challenged wanted to fight with eight-foot-long log poles or big chunks of rock. It jest weren't refined.

Perhaps the best-known duel back then was in 1827 when a feller in one of the two duels that day missed his opponent and hit one of the specktators by mistake. Unfortunately for him, the bystander was Jim Bowie, who did not take kindly to being shot.

Ol' Jim pulled out his famous bowie knife, rushed over, and stabbed the feller who had shot him. The duelist cracked Jim over the head with his empty dueling pistol, bringing him down to his knees. Somebody else shot Jim Bowie again — and then th' whole thing turned into a brawl. Jim was gettin' a might riled and fought like a wildcat.

The brawl only lasted ten minutes.

When it was over, there was two men dead and four men seriously injured. Jim Bowie had been shot several times and stabbed through the chest with a sword. And he had a severe head injury from being cracked with that dueling pistol. But he were a tough ol' boy, and he had won his fight. Jim recovered and went on to fight many more times and be kilt at th' Alamo years later.

But this ain't the story about Jim Bowie. This is about the Kaintuck blacksmith an' the Frenchman.

Now there was this hillbilly blacksmith from Kentucky who come to Louisiana an' set up his business. He were a powerful good blacksmith, an' could make a lot more money in New Orleans than he could back in the mountains.

He were a great giant of a man, standing well over six-and-a-half feet tall, with strong an' massive hands. But for all that, he were a gentle soul and friendly as a hound dog.

But one day, the big man happened to say something in public that offended this particular feisty Frenchman. So th' Frenchman challenged the Kaintuck to a duel. The blacksmith was a kind an' gentle soul, an' he didn't know quite what to make of it.

The Frenchman stood only about 5 feet 4 inches tall in his boots, but he was the master swordsman of all New Orleans — the fencing master who taught lessons to the French and Spanish aristocracy. He were a very dangerous opponent.

"Aw, shucks, I don't wanna fight the little feller," said the blacksmith. "He ain't never done nothin' wrong to me. I'll just apologize and have done with it."

But his friends explained to him that New Orleans society didn't work that way. There was the code of honor to be considered. If the blacksmith was to turn down th' challenge, he would be called a coward and would be ostrich-sized in the community. Nobody would come to his blacksmith shop and he would go broke.

"Ya gotta fight this here Frenchman whether you like to or not," said his pals.

So the Kaintuck thought it over for a while. Since he was the challenged party, he got to choose the weapons and the place for the fight.

When the Frenchman's pals showed up at the smithy — they called them "seconds" fer some reason — they wanted to arrange the details for the fight. What were to be th' weapons an' where was the duel to take place?

The Kaintuck Blacksmith gave it to 'em straight:

"Blacksmith hammers — six feet deep in Lake Pontchartrain."

The two aristocrats looked astonished. This was unheard of.

The blacksmith was tall enough to stand in six feet of water, but the French fencing master would be in over his head. And he couldn't begin to lift a heavy blacksmith hammer.

"Wal, I'm the challenged party," said the blacksmith. "I get to choose weapons an' the place fer the fight. You turnin' down my terms?"

The two Frenchmen looked at each other an' said that they would report his terms to the fencing master. But they were afraid what would happen. The fiery fencing master was known to have a hot temper.

But when his seconds relayed the blacksmith's terms, the little fencing master broke out into hearty laughter.

"Zat ees ze funniest thing I have ever heard in my life!" he chortled. "It is evident that I have misjudged zis blacksmith. He has ze most brilliant sense of humor I have ever encountered!"

The Kaintuck blacksmith an' the Frenchman fencing master became th' best of friends — an' they both lived happily ever after.

Sharpshooter Zeke

WILBUR: You know, talkin' about guns — I once heard of a feller in Saint Louis who would bet you $5,000 that if you tossed a silver dollar into the air, he could shoot and hit it before it hit the ground three times out of five.

ZEKE: Oh, yeah?

WILBUR: Yes, and he'd also bet you the same amount that if you held that dollar coin between your teeth, he could shoot it out of your mouth three times out of five. He even had a cowboy sidekick who was willing to put the coin in his mouth and let him shoot at it.

ZEKE: Well, I don't see anything so wonderful about that. Only three times out of five? Why, I could shoot that coin and hit it *every time.*

WILBUR: *Every time?*

ZEKE: Every single blessed time. I wish I'd know'd about that feller. I'd have bet with him and won that $5,000. And I'd have used one of these modern little dollar coins at that, not a big huge old silver dollar.

WILBUR: How could you *possibly* hit a little coin like that *every time?*

ZEKE: Very simple. — I'd use a sawed-off shotgun...

The Halloween Outhouse

There was a story told about Zeke Jaochum back when he was jess a boy. One Halloween, as a prank, Zeke sneaked outta the house in the middle o' the night an' tipped the old outhouse over the cliff down inta the crick.

It went clatterin' an' crashin' down the embankment an' lit with a splash in the muddy water.

Next day, Zeke's ol' daddy grab him by the collar an' askt him if he had dumped over the outhouse.

"But before yew answer, Zeke, remember th' story o' George Washington an' the cherry tree.

"George Washington told the truth to his daddy, and he was not punished. Now boy, did yew tip over that outhouse?"

Zeke said, "Father, I cannot tell a lie. I tipped over th' outhouse..."

Whereupon his ol' daddy whupped him good an' solid with a stout hickory stick.

"BUT DADDY! You said George Washington told th' truth about th' cherry tree and warn't punished."

Zeke's ol' daddy sez: "George Washington's daddy warn't sittin' in th' gosh dern cherry tree at the time!"

PART THREE

The Frost Haint of 'Possum Hollow and Other Ozark Tales

The Frost Haint of 'Possum Hollow

Back in the old days, there was a settlement up by Hookrum's Mountain, jist around the bend from Piney Ridge, that was known as 'Possum Hollow. On the edge of the town, off by itself about halfway up a wooded slope, there was a deserted roadhouse known as the Old McCann Place. The surroundin' trees had all died of blight, the well went sour, and the old house had a wicked reputation. No one had lived there since the last of the McCanns was all killed off some time after the Civil War. The place was said to be hainted.

Now, it warn't no ordinary specter that wandered the halls and bedrooms of the old inn — it was a Frost Haint. It had long slippery arms like the leg bone of a cow, icy white hair, green glowin' eyes, blue icicles hangin' from its shoulders, and frosty breath that was cold as death. Whenever anyone tried to sleep in the big bed of the best room at the Old McCann Place, the Frost Haint would come creepin' up out of the cellars in the deep of night and into the room where the sleeper was layin'. Then it would blow its dreadawfulsome cold breath into the poor unfortunate's face, and come next morning that person would be found froze to death.

Folks jist didn't go near the Old McCann Place no more.

Now my wife's Uncle Elmer was a gentle man. He was a likable sort of feller, but he had a few personal habits that you might call a bit antisocial. Accordingly, he never stayed for very long in any one place. He made his living by trappin' fur, so he spent most of his time in the wilds.

Uncle Elmer 'specially loved Hog Jowl Hash, which he made accordin' to his own recipe, usin' lots of garlic, hot Mexican peppers, and strong horseradish — all topped off with a big hunk of ripe limburger. For desert, he'd chaw on a big garlic clove the way other folks might eat an apple. Then he'd go to sleep under the stars, wrapped up in a big mummy-sack that he'd sewed up out of bear skins.

After Uncle Elmer had finished trappin' for the winter, sold his whole season's worth of furs, and was flush with money, he liked to get hisself a nice soft bed and sleep indoors for a change. So he did.

Well, sir. One particular night a few years back, Uncle Elmer found hisself at Wilbur Pooley's cabin up in 'Possum Hollow. He and some of the other boys had been playin' checkers by the fire and sippin' on some of Wilbur's hot cider.

Of course, there warn't no hotels anywheres near 'Possum Hollow, so finally Uncle Elmer spoke up and said, "Boys, do any of you know any place hereabouts where a tired man can git his-self a great soft bed with warm quilts and real feather pillows?"

"Wal, thar's the Old McCann Place," said Pete Rickman. "It's the only house this side of Hookrum's Mountain got them kinda things. But you don't wanta sleep up thar — the place is hainted!"

"Oh, well, I don't care nothin' about haints," said Uncle Elmer. "Long as I got a nice place to lay mah head."

Despite the warnings from the other men, Uncle Elmer packed up his gear and lit out for the Old McCann Place. The ground was still hard-packed from winter, and the black branches of dead trees loomed dark in the fog. The old roadhouse looked ghastly with the pale moon shinin' behind it through the mist.

But inside, Uncle Elmer found that the windows was all tight, the floors and walls was solid, and the furniture was covered with old sheets to keep off the dust. *A right cozy place, with a little dustin' up,* he thought to hisself. *Especially since its free of charge.* Uncle Elmer built a nice fire in the kitchen cookstove and rustled up a big spicy batch of Hog Jowl Hash — throwin' in a dozen extra cloves of garlic, jist for good measure. It were a memorable meal.

Then he climbed up the stairs and picked out the biggest and best room in the house, built hisself a fire, and tucked into sleep under a pile of quilts and goose-down comforters. No sooner did his head touch the big feather pillow than Uncle Elmer was snorin' like a ring-tailed roarer.

Well, it was jist midnight when the Frost Haint creeped out of the cellars and across the stone kitchen floor. The fire in the cookstove went out with its passin'. It stalked through the front room and up the stairs. Hoarfrost formed on the window glazings. It clumped down the hallway, its icicles clackin' like iron chains. Then it come into the room where Uncle Elmer was sleepin'. The fireplace went out. The Frost Haint come over to the bedside and reached out its long, cold, slippery arms....

Now Uncle Elmer was accustomed to sleepin' in the wilderness. Many's the time he'd had bears and paynters come up on him in the night while he was asleep. So the minute that haint's cold fingers touched the quilt, why that old trapper was awake and fightin' like a wildcat. The Frost Haint's arms was powerful strong, but Uncle Elmer rasseled him. He was gettin' a might riled. Then the Frost Haint took a deep breath and blew its cold, icy frost right into Uncle Elmer's face.

Uncle Elmer inhaled and *blew his breath* into the Frost Haint's face.

You shoulda seen that spider-legged old skeleton skidaddle!! That Frost Haint ain't never been seen since. Uncle Elmer enjoyed the best night's sleep he'd had in many years.

Brewer's Mule

Now my Grandpa Brewer was a fine woodcarver, he was. I can see him to this day, sittin' on the front porch whittlin' his wood. Sometimes it was oak or walnut, and other times maybe cherry or mahogany or zebrawood. He claimed there warn't no art to it; he said all you had to do to make a statue of somethin' was to take a hunk of wood and scrape off all the part that didn't look like what you was a-carvin'. Anyhow, he made dogs and cats and sometimes a deer, and when he'd finished he'd sand it right smooth so it was a real pleasure to look on.

One day when I was about ten or twelve, he carved me a egg outta rosewood. Where he got that hunk of rosewood I never knowed, but he carved on it all afternoon, and I seen him do it. The egg was about the size of a goose egg and was a deep red-dish-brown. After he'd carved and sanded it, he rubbed it with oil by hand so it had a fine finish to it like it was varnished — and smooth as glass. It was so perfect you could spin it on end jist like a real egg, it was so balanced. Then he give it to me, and I've had it ever since. Livy uses it now sometimes to darn socks on, but when I was a boy I jist carried it in my pocket.

Anyhow, whilst Grandpa Brewer was a-carvin' the egg I sat and watched him, and he told me a tale about when he was young and free and happened to come across a mule. Grandpa was about seventeen at the time and was walkin' along a dirt road one day in June. He warn't out for any particular purpose to speak of, he was jist walkin' — when he happened to come across a mule standin' there by the roadside with its tail tied to a tree.

The critter jist stood there with its tail stickin' straight out behind with about five feet of hemp rope betwixt it and an old oak tree. Grandpa studied the beast a spell, and then went over to a feller who was sittin' by the roadside, restin' on a rock and sippin' corn mash from a stone jug.

Grandpa said as how he'd allow that the feller had the mule strung-up proper and all, but that it was beyond him the reason *why* the mule was trussed so. The feller took another sip of his corn mash and told Grandpa that he was a philosopher. He'd been a-considerin' the rel'tive merits of beasts versus them of plants, and he decided to have a contest to find out which was the better. He said he'd thought on it for a long while, and finally determined the way to do it was to have a tug-o'-war betwixt a mule and a tree. Grandpa looked at the feller a minute and then looked at the mule, who was standin' there, peaceful-like, blinkin' its eyes and twitchin' the skin on its rump to dislodge the blueflies.

Then Grandpa said that was all well and good, but how in the hell was he goin' to tell when one or t'other had *won*. The feller jumped up, walked over to the mule, and pointed to a line drawn in the dirt halfway betwixt the mule and the tree. He said whichever one drug t'other across the line *first* would be the winner — and all he'd have to do was to watch the line.

Grandpa Brewer asked the feller what made him think a tree would want to drag a mule across a line. The feller said if the tree didn't have enough gumption to try, why it was likely inferior and deserved to lose.

Grandpa studied the feller a minute longer, looked at the mule, looked at the tree. Then Grandpa asked the feller if he'd consider *placin' a little wager* on the outcome. Well, sir, that feller's hairy face broke out into a fat grin and he said he might consider it, dependin' on what the stakes was. Grandpa said he'd put up his silver watch that the tree would win. The feller examined the watch and said he reckoned he could put up his Kentucky long-rifle agin it. Grandpa said he'd have to see the rifle first, seein' as how the watch was Swiss-made and had a genuine cylinder escapement.

The feller said he'd fetch the gun from his house, which was jist up the road on t'other side. Soon as the feller'd left to get it, Grandpa waited till he was out of sight around the bend, and then carefully rubbed out the line in the dirt with his boot, smoothed it over a mite, and then made a new line a few feet in front of the mule. When the feller come back with the rifle, Grandpa said it would do, and the feller asked how the contest was a-comin'.

Well, sir, Grandpa Brewer said, the mule had been winnin' for a time, but for the last few minutes the tree had been puttin' up a terrible struggle, and it would be hard to say how matters presently stood. The feller said he'd go check and see — and he found to his dismay that the mule was now on the losin' side of the line, standin' there and blinkin' its eyes at him sorrowfully.

So Grandpa won the rifle. And the feller give him the mule, too, sayin' what the heck good was a critter that couldn't even out-pull a tree? So Grandpa Brewer got the rifle and the mule. He didn't need 'em both. He figgered if he kept them both, he might accidentally shoot the mule with the rifle. So he decided to sell one of them. If he sold the mule, he could hunt with the rifle, but Grandpa hated to hunt. If he sold the gun, he could ride to town on the mule to buy food, and wouldn't need to hunt. So Grandpa sold the rifle to a man over in Sheldahl for twelve dollars and used the money to buy hay for the mule, which he kept till the day it died.

Grandpa said he never did feel sorry about havin' fooled that feller. He said, if the Good Lord hadn't intended for that feller to get tricked, he'd-a either give him some brains in the first place — *or else moved the tree.*

Gowrows

Now the gowrow was an extraordinary reptile that terrorized the Ozark Mountains back in the 1880s. It were a lizard-like beast some twenty feet long with enormous tusks, short legs, and webbed feet with long, sharp claws on each toe. The gowrow's body was covered with green scales, and its back bristled with short spikes. The tail was long and thin, with a pointed, blade-shaped formation at the end. It had big, sharp teeth.

The gowrow hatched its young from soft-shelled eggs the size of beer kegs, and the females carried the newly hatched younguns in a pouch like a 'possum. Gowrows devour all manner of deer, cattle, sheep, goats, and the occasional Presbyterian.

Old Pete Woolsey, who used to run a fair decent restaurant in the Ozarks down by Bentonville, believed in the scientific likelihood that gowrows survived well up into the 1920s — and was a might put out if city folks scoffed at the notion.

"I don't see nothin' so unreasonable about it," he declared. "Them scientists over at the State University are tellin' people that there used to be elephants right here in Arkansas. *Elephants*, mind you, with red wool on 'em two foot long!"

"Well, that's different," said the city slicker. "That was thousands of years ago."

"Would you rather believe them professors, talkin' about red elephants in the Ozarks before America was even *discovered*, than believe my Grandpaw's story of what happened in his own lifetime?"

"Listen, Pete, did your grandfather ever *see* a gowrow?"

"No, he didn't. I never seen a paynter, neither. But lots of old-timers did see paynters, an' killed 'em, too, right here in this country. I've listened at them hunters a-talkin', an' there

ain't no doubt in my mind that there was plenty of paynters here in the early days. My grandpaw heerd about the gowrows, jist like I've heerd about paynters."

Pete began to look a might indignant, as if the city feller had inplied that his granddaddy was a liar. Pete Woolsey was not a man to offend, so the city slicker offered to buy him a drink or two — and they said no more about gowrows.

Some years back, a feller in Missouri claimed to have captured a gowrow alive. He had somehow persuaded the critter to devour a whole wagon-load of dried apples. This made the varmint powerful thirsty, and once it had drank three or eight barrels full of water, it swelled up so big it couldn't fit back into its cave. The feller exhibited it in a tent, charging twenty-five cents admission. Outside the tent, he had a horridsome painting of the monster devouring a poor family of farmers.

When a sizable crowd of spectators was seated on the benches inside the tent, there come a dreadawfulsome roaring noise from backstage, the sound of several gunshots, some crashes, and clanking chains. Then the showman staggered out in front of the audience with his clothes torn to shreds and his face covered with blood.

"Run for your lives!" he yelled. "The gowrow has broke loose!"

Jist then, the whole back of the tent collapsed amid more thunderous roars, the sounds of chains breaking, and people screaming. The spectators lit out for the woods like their britches was on fire — *not even stopping to get their money back.*

The Cracked Pot

Back in the old days, there was a mountaineer up by Rumpus Ridge who lived to be nigh on a hundred years old. His wife had died and all his children moved on — except for his youngest daughter, Penelope. The gal took good care of her old daddy, cookin' for him and cleanin' the cabin. Each morning, she would go down to the spring to fetch water. She carried an old ox-yoke across her shoulders with a heavy earthenware pot hung by ropes from each end. She'd fill the two pots right up to their brims with clear, sparklin' springwater, and then she'd trudge her heavy load back up the winding trail to the cabin. First, she'd give her old daddy a long, cool drink of water, and then she'd use the rest to wash up the dishes, scrub mop the floor, and clean the windows.

These two remarkable pots was big and heavy — they held five gallons apiece. Now one of the pots was fine and whole, with a shiny glaze and a speckled finish. Day after day it always delivered a full passel of springwater to the cabin. But t'other pot had a crack in it. Twarn't a big crack, but it was long and thin, runnin' half-way down the side and across the bottom. The cracked pot always leaked a small trickle during the long trek up from the spring to the cabin, and arrived only half-full. Penelope always used up the water from the cracked pot first, so's it wouldn't leak all over the floor of the cabin.

Now the fine pot was prideful and vain; it boasted about its beautiful finish and all the water it brought to the cabin. It made hurtful remarks about the pot with the crack, callin' it lazy and wasteful. The poor old pot was ashamed of its imperfection, and was miserable that it could only accomplish half of what it was originally capable of doin'.

Finally, after eight years of bitter failure, the pot with the crack finally spoke to Penelope. "Gal, I owe you an apology. I am ashamed of myself — I've failed you."

"Why for land's sake!" said Penelope. "What on earth have you got to be ashamed of?"

"For the last eight years, I've never once't been able to carry my full load. This crack in my side causes me to leak water all the way back to your old daddy's cabin. Because of my flaw, you have to do extra work. I'm not pullin' my fair share of the load."

Penelope looked fondly at the old cracked pot, which had belonged to her great-grandmother, and then was passed down through the family for over two-hundred years. "Next time we go down to the spring," she said, "I want you to notice the trail. Tell me what you see."

Next mornin' when they went to the spring, the cracked old pot noticed beautiful mountain wildflowers blooming along the path. But then, when they got back to the cabin, the old pot was dismayed, for it had once again lost half its water on the return trip.

Penelope said to the pot, "Did you happen to notice those flowers growing on the side of the trail? Did you notice that they *are only growing on your side of the path?* Not on the other pot's side? That's because I knew about your flaw and took advantage of it. I planted wildflowers along your side of the path, and each day when we walk back from the spring, you've watered those flowers. For the last eight years, I have been able to pick beautiful flowers to decorate my old daddy's dinner table and to put cut flowers on all the windowsills. Without you being jist the way you are, we would not of had all this beauty to grace our home..."

Now there is a moral to this story: *sometimes even us crackpots serve a useful purpose.*

The Granddaddy Paynter

Now back when the *Flora Jones* first come up the Osage River to Harmony Mission, Missouri, in the spring of 1844, there was one of the old settlers plowing his field when he heard the most bodacious awful sound he'd ever experienced in his whole life. It was a long, wailing cry and an angry roaring — like some kind of terrible beast. This is a true story. The mountaineer grabbed his rifle and lit out on his mule to warn the folks in nearby Papinsville.

Well, as you may know, there was all manner of awesomeful monsters in the Ozark Mountains back then. There was the paynter, the gowrow, the jimplicute, the nighbehind, the kingdoodle and the gollywog, the whangdoodle, the willipus-wallipus, and the snawfus — to name jist a few. So naturally, this mountaineer figgered it must be the granddaddy of all dreadawfulsome paynters. He shouted for the townfolk to grab their shotguns, turn loose the dogs, and lock up the women and babies. The terrible shriek of the creature was heard in town by now, and folks said it was a gigantic beast of some unheard-of species from the Rocky Mountains or some such God-forsaken region.

One of the young girls had jist gone down to the river to fetch water — in the very direction the sounds of the monster was coming from. Her daddy and a bunch of the menfolk dashed down to the river and fetched her back to safety.

The dogs was strangely unable to detect any odor from the approaching varmint, but the awful creature was getting closer by the minute. They could hear it puffing and blowing and thrashing water as it made its way along the riverbank, roaring like thunder and emitting ear-piercing shrieks. This was far worse than any monster ever heard of in Ozark folklore. The hunters cocked their rifles and made ready to deal with this frightful beast.

Well, you can imagine their astonishment went the *Flora Jones* steamed around the bend in the river. These folks had never seen a steamboat before.

Mad Wolf Mike

Back in the old days, there was a bartender name of Jim O'Grady come to the Ozarks from out East and took a job at Rumpus Ridge. Now this was not the place down in Benton County, Arkansas, referred to as Rumpus Ridge— nor yet was it the town up north of Galena, Missouri, which is sometimes called by that name.

This was the *original* Rumpus Ridge — right here in the heart of the Ozarks over by Hookrum's Mountain. It was a rough-and-ready neighborhood, a bit turbulent, and rowdy at times.

Now the owner of the Bingbuffer Tavern in Rumpus Ridge was a fat, jovial feller by the name of P.T. McQuary, who had a grin as wide as the Missouri River. "You ever worked in a rough saloon before, young feller?" McQuary asked Jim O'Grady.

"Well, I worked for twenty years at a waterfront dive in New Jersey," said Jim to his perspective boss. "We had a lot of drunken sailors and longshoremen. If I could handle that lot, I can handle most anything, sir."

"Wal, things is a might different here in the Ozarks," said McQuary. "Now, most of the boys are okay — they git a little rambunctious on Friday and Saturday nights. But I'm sure you can handle that. Sometimes the feudin' clans are in town on the same night and there's a bit of shootin' and bloodshed, but you can handle that, too.

"But now listen to me, son, and you listen good." McQuary's face went pale as a 'possum's belly. "If *Mad Wolf Mike* ever comes to town, you jist do what he says. Don't cross him. Give him whatever he wants at no charge. You git me, boy?"

"Yes, sir...," said Jim.

Well, Jim O'Grady started workin' at the Bingbuffer Tavern the next day. Most of the work was fairly simple. A few loafers would hang around on lazy afternoons, and Sam Hookrum, the town drunk, would sleep it off behind the piano. Sometimes bootleggers would deliver moonshine or chock to the back door.

The fights on Friday and Saturday nights was no worse than what Jim was used to back East, although the Buford feuds was a might taxin' even for a man with Jim's background. But life in the mountains was clean an' invigoratin' — and Jim O'Grady found his new life to be right tolerable.

Then one hot afternoon in August, Grover Finch rushed into the Bingbuffer Tavern and hollered, "Hoof it, boys! *Mad Wolf Mike's comin' to town!*"

Well, sir — you jist should have seen those tangle-foot loafers clear out of there. Arms scrambling, legs pumping, and hats flyin' in the air and left behind in the dust. Sam Hookrum woke with a start and climbed up the chimney. Even the McCarty brothers, who weighed 240 pounds apiece, hoofed it out of town like their hair was on fire and their britches was catchin'. Outside, mothers was takin' little children off the streets; dogs was barkin' and lightin' out for the tall timber. The Buford boys

was loadin' their whole clan into a wagon and hitchin' up the mules; soon they was gone in a cloud of dust. Then everything was quiet.

There was not a soul left in the town of Rumpus Ridge but Jim O'Grady.

Then the ground began to shake. There was the thunderin' sound of something in the distance comin' closer. Then come a blood-chillin' scream like a hundred wildcats: *YEEE—HAAAW!* Around the corner by Basswood's Livery Stable come the biggest, hairiest, meanest-lookin' mountain man that Jim O'Grady had ever seen in his life. The mountaineer was ridin' with one foot on a grizzly bear and t'other on a buffalo. He had a paynter around his neck like a collar and was whippin' his mounts on, whoopin' and hollerin' and usin' a rattlesnake for a whip.

The feller pulled up at the hitchin' post, jumped down to the ground, and punched the bear and the buffalo each square between the eyes, knockin' them senseless. He bit the head off the rattlesnake and pitched it in the ditch. He grabbed the paynter by its tail, swung it over his head three times, and flung it onto the roof. Then he hitched up his belt and stalked into the tavern.

"I want a drink!!" he said, crashin' his fist down on the bar and splinterin' the woodwork. Jim fetched him a mug full of white lightning. The mountaineer grabbed the mug and crashed it out through the window. "I SAID I WANT A DRINK! — NOT JIST A THIMBLEFUL!"

He grabbed the whole gallon stone jug out of Jim's hand and drained all that moonshine whiskey at one pull.

"W-would you like another drink, sir?" stammered the bartender.

"Heck, no," said the mountaineer, wipin' his mouth with the back of his hairy hand. "I gotta clear out of here —

"Mad Wolf Mike's comin' to town!"

Jesse James and the Hog Meat

Now there was once a feller by the name of Charlie Hayden went to a hog scaldin' over at Coon Hollow, where he met the purdiest, sweetest, dumbest gal this side of Arkansas. Her name was Matilda Clemons. Charlie courted her, proposed to her, and married her all on the same day. Then he put Matilda on the seat of his wagon, loaded up the hog he'd bought, and headed for home.

When they got back to his soddy over on Hookrum's Mountain, Charlie set to butcherin', dryin', and smokin' the hog. Matilda watched him work — but she didn't understand a bit of it.

Finally, when the meat was done, Charlie put all the ribs and backbone on the west wall of the smokehouse and said to Matilda, "Now look here, my darlin'. Them is for our present needs." He nodded at the ribs and backbone. "You understand, gal?"

"Yep! Prezinsneeds," said Matilda — but she didn't understand a bit of it.

Then Charlie hung all the shanks and ham over on the east wall of the smokehouse and said to Matilda, "Now look here, my darlin'. Them is for bye-and-bye." He nodded at the shanks and ham. "You got that?"

"Yep!! Bymeby," said Matilda — but she didn't understand a bit of it.

Then Charlie put all the sausages, souse, and bacon on the north wall, and told Matilda, "Them sausages and bacon is for afterwards." He nodded at the meat.

"Yep! Arturwards," said Matilda. She was a very agreeable gal by nature — but she didn't understand a bit of it.

Charlie Hayden said to Matilda, "Now look here, my darlin'. I gotta ride down to Kimberling Ferry for a few days. You mind the homestead while I'm gone." He kissed his bride, mounted up on his mule, and rode out.

Matilda swept up the cabin and did chores. She pumped water from the well, washed the bedding, and milked the goat. Next day, she was a-settin' in the kitchen knittin' a blanket, when who should come ridin' up the trail but Jesse James hisself.

Ol' Jesse was havin' a busy week. His gang had jist robbed a Union Pacific train, three banks, and a Yankee they'd met on the road outside Springfield. The Pinkerton agents was hot on their tails, so Jesse decided it would be a wise idea to hide out in the Ozark hills until the heat was off. He and the boys was on their way to a limestone cave near Monegaw that they used as a hideout, and they was all camped nearby.

Jesse was in high spirits, and was singin' the old ballad "Price and Snead", a Civil War ditty about General Sterling Price and his adjutant, Colonel Thomas Snead, who was both prominent Confederates on the western border durin' the late war.

> Oh, I come from down in Dixie, with Price and Snead I roam;
> For I'm jist a Rebel soldier, and I'm very far from home.
> I eat when I am thirsty, I drink when I am dry;
> If the Yankee boys don't kill me, then I'll live until I die.
>
> Price and Snead, Price and Snead — no matter where you roam;
> I come from down in Dixie and the Ozarks are my home.

"Price and Snead, Price and Snead...," sang ole Jesse as he rode along the trail.

"Prisensneed?" Matilda said to herself. "Why, this must be Prisensneed — the very man that the ribs and backbone is for!" So she opened the door and hollered at Jesse. "HEY! Is you-uns the feller Pricensneed?"

Ol' Jesse reigned up and scratched his head in puzzlement. Truth be told, he'd jist been ponderin' whether there was anythin' worth robbin' this little farm for. Finally, he sez, "Why, yes, ma'am. That I am. Price and Snead."

"Wal, mister," she allowed, "yer meat is out back in the smokehouse."

Jesse didn't quite know what to make of Matilda, so he jist sat there on his horse. Finally, the gal said, "Come on, I'll fetch it for you." Jesse followed Matilda around to the smokehouse, where she began luggin' out the smoked ribs and backbone meat, loadin' it into a poke on Jesse's horse.

This was by far the easiest loot ol' Jesse James had ever come by. As Matilda hefted the last of the meat onto his horse, she said, "Hey, Mister Prisensneed — iffen you should happen to see Mister Bymeby, tell him his meat's ready, too. But ask him to bring his own poke, cuz I ain't got no more."

Now Jesse James was no man's fool. He rode hard back to the big oak tree where his brother Frank was camped with Cole Younger. "Frank!" Jesse sez. "Git yerself to that sod house up the trail and tell that pretty gal that yer name is Mister Bymeby."

So Frank James rode up to Charlie Hayden's soddy, and in no time a-tall Matilda had loaded him down with shanks and ham. "Hey, mister," she said. "You-uns ain't by any chance seen Mister Arturwards, have ye? I got meat for him, too."

Naturally, Jesse James sent Cole Younger to the farm claimin' to be Mister Arturwards. Matilda was happy to load him up with all the smoked sausages, bacon, and souse. The James-Younger Gang feasted well that night. Next morning, they figgered that they better move on to their hideout cave, so they went to fetch their loot from where they'd hid it.

Jist about the same time, Charlie Hayden got back from Kimberling Ferry. Matilda rushed out to meet him, she was so prideful of what she'd accomplished. "I done give all that meat to them three fellers — jist like you told me to!" she said.

"What!" shouted her husband. Charlie ran out to the smoke-house and found all his meat was gone. He stomped and roared and threw a reg'lar ring-tailed fit. He was madder than wet hornets. Finally, Charlie hollered, "We gotta find them varmints! Listen, my darlin' — smother the fire and pull the door to! Then foller me!"

Charlie dashed off like a rabbit with a paynter on its tail. Matilda muttered to herself: smother the fire — *humpf!* Wouldn't it be easier to pour water on it than t' smother it? But Matilda was an obedient wife, so she took a blanket off Charlie's bed and shoved it down over the mouth of the fireplace. When the fire was "smothered", she wrapped the smolderin' coals into what was left of the blanket and tried to remember what she was supposed to do next. Foller Charlie. Pull the door, too. *Hmmn.*

Matilda stuffed the rag full of burnin' embers into her big apron pocket and then used the kitchen knife to pry the leather hinge straps off the front door of the cabin. Then she set out to follow Charlie, and pulled the door, too.

Charlie was followin' the trail of the horses' hoofprints when Matilda caught up to him, draggin' the cabin door behind her. Sooner than you'da thunkit, they come to the robber camp. Jist then, Jesse and the boys come back from diggin' up their gold.

Charlie took one look at them and dern near swallowed his heart. "Land-o'-Goshen, my darlin'! That's Jesse James and his gang! Quick — climb up the tree." Ever the dutiful wife, Matilda clambered up the old oak tree after her husband, and pulled the door, too. (She still didn't understand a bit of it).

Jesse and Frank James and Cole Younger set down under the tree and started pullin' money out of their coats and emptyin' their trouser pockets into a big pile so's they could divvy up the loot.

Now it is a little-known fact that, although they was robbers and killers, the James Gang had a religious bent. Even as a child, Jesse would rise up in church to ask the congregation to pray for his brother's soul — and he was baptized right after his gang robbed the Daviess County Savings Bank up in Gallatin.

Cole Younger sang in the choir of his Baptist church. So what happened next is not as surprising as it mighta been otherwise.

Ol' Jesse was laughin' and chawin' on a piece of jerky while he counted out the gold. "That gal was purdy as a picture, but she shore was dumb!" he said. "Why, if she could see us right now, she'd rain hot coals on our heads!"

Jist about that time, the hot coals in Matilda's apron burned through, and down from that big old oak tree they come in a burnin' shower — right on the heads of the James Gang!

Cole Younger jumped up and hollered, "It's the Judgment Day!"

There was quite a commotion amongst the robbers as they danced around in that hail of glowin' hot coals, yellin' and jumpin' and tryin' to slap out their burnin' shirts.

"Oh, Lordy!" screamed Frank James. And Jesse was shakin' like a leaf.

Cole Younger stood with his arms at his sides and his eyes bulgin'. "Next thing you know, boys," he intoned in a dreadawfulsome voice, "the very Door of Heaven will open!"

About that time, Charlie Hayden's front door come a-crashin' down through the branches and limbs of that big old oak tree, with sticks and leaves a-whirlin' every which way.

Well, you jist shoulda seen them outlaws cut outa there! They was a-runnin' like the British after the Battle of New Orleans — through the briars and the brambles and the bushes where a rabbit couldn't go! They run so fast that they left the gold behind them, and kept on runnin' till the sun come up the next morning. So they did.

Charlie Hayden and Matilda climbed down from the big oak tree. Charlie took Jesse James' horse and Matilda rode Frank's, and they tied the saddlebags full of treasure to Cole Younger's horse, along with all the meats and the cabin's front door.

As they was a-ridin' home, Charlie turned to his bride. "Now look here, my darlin'. I ain't complainin' none. But next time some feller comes to the door wantin' meat — could you mebbe ask him to *pay in advance?*"

Doc Martin and the Silver Bullets

Now some folks have lots of money and some folks don't; that jist seems to be the way o' the world — but it do seem a dern shame that you and me ain't got a whole lot more'n we do. But what's even sadder is when a nice feller like Doc Martin (who was fairly well off to start with) sacrifices everything he's got to go off chasin' after some wild and crazy dream of strikin' it rich.

Of all the folks here in Dover, Doc Martin was one of the most successful, respected, and best-liked fellers in the community. He delivered my boy Aaron and all eight of my sister Molly's kids. Fact be told, he'd delivered most near every young'un born in this part of Arkansas since 1893.

The Doc was as sensible, hardworking, and dependable as the best of 'em — up till the autumn of 1905, that is. His troubles all began when he decided to take some time off from his work to go deer huntin'. Doc had always been so busy takin' care of sick folks and deliverin' babies that he hadn't been able to get away to hunt for over three years.

He had on his bookshelf a little sack of rifle shells he'd taken as barter payment from Tobe Inmon back in 1903. Tobe was a surly Kaintuck who lived in a cabin about twelve miles north of Dover, up by Moccasin Creek Valley. Folks said he'd been run out of Appalachia for rustlin' cattle. He was a ragged and dirty ol' recluse who rarely spoke to anyone when he come to town — and that weren't often. From time-to-time, he'd bring some rangy chickens or a half-wild hog in to the Trading Post to barter for sugar, flour, and such-like. He lived in a decrepit little shanty he'd built hisself, along with his dismal-lookin' wife and a passel of wretched chilluns. Tobe's youngest boy was took with the fever, and Doc Martin saved his life.

When he got up there, the doctor was appalled at the primitive livin' and poverty at the Inmon homestead. It was jist like ol' Doc that he wasn't even gonna charge the poor folks anything for saving their son. He told Tobe that he could settle up when things got better. But Tobe insisted on payin' his debt — and offered the Doc a sack of large-caliber bullets as payment. Now this was back at a time when ammunition was scarce as hen's teeth, and the Doc accepted 'em right gladly. They was fine-lookin' bullets, too, and Doc Martin asked Tobe where he'd got 'em.

"Wal, ah jist made 'em mah ownself," said Tobe Inman. "Ah foun' sum lead in a ol' mine in the woods back o' mah cabin."

"I thank you kindly," said Doc Martin as he packed the little sack of shells away in his carriage. "I'll use them when I go deer huntin' this fall."

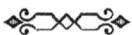

O' course, as I mentioned before, Doc didn't get around to deer huntin' for a couple years after that. Then, while he was gettin' his huntin' gear ready, he fetched the sack of shells from the

bookcase in his study where he'd stashed 'em after he got home from Tobe's. Doc put the sack on his desk so's he wouldn't forget to take 'em along the next morning.

That evening, Doc Martin was a-readin' a book at his desk when he picked up one of the shells to diddle in his fingers. Presently, he commenced to pickin' at the black residue on the bullet with his fingernail. As the tarnish was scratched off, he noticed a shiny color underneath — kinda like silver!

Mighty peculiar, that. The next day, Doc decided to cancel his huntin' trip. Instead, he took the bullets to a mineralogist pal over in Russellville. 'Twarn't no surprise when the whole dern lot of bullets turned out to be made of pure silver. Doc Martin sold the sack of shells for seventy-two dollars cash. Quite a good payment for a doctor's house call in them days!

That night, ol' Doc dreamed of a fortune in silver hid away in some cave back of Tobe's place. Next day, he whipped his horse and buggy over the rocky road to Moccasin Creek Valley. But when he pulled up at the cabin — weren't nobody to home. The place was deserted. Neighbor folks told Doc that Tobe had packed up and absquatulated six months earlier. Said he'd gone to Texas.

Doc Martin climbed the low hill back of Tobe's cabin and wandered through the woods. He examined every rock and hollow, every nook and cranny — but he couldn't find a trace of that silver. Finally, darkness fell and Doc had to come back home to Dover.

Next morning, he provisioned hisself for an extended camping and headed back to Moccasin Creek Valley. For nigh on two-and-a-half weeks, he lived up there in that decrepit ramshackle cabin. Up the airy mountains and down the misty glens he tromped in search of Tobe Inmon's lost silver mine. O' course, if a disreputable Kaintuck had told *me* he got his metal from an old cave back of his cabin, that woulda been the *last place* I'da thunk to look for it. But ol' Doc was always such a trusting soul.

Exhausted, filthy, and unshaven, ol' Doc come back to Dover lookin' as reprehensible as old Tobe Inmon hisself! He grew mysterious and secretive. He ignored his medical practice and spent all his time makin' preparations for another treasure hunt expedition. Doc Martin come to be a fanatic, consumed with the very notion of findin' the lost silver.

Over the next few years, ol' Doc made numerous forays into the hills lookin' for that lost silver mine. His patients gave up on him and took to seein' other doctors. Doc Martin ran out of money. He sold his house and practice to finance his treasure hunts. He pursued his vision with an insane passion, and folks in Dover whispered that he'd gone mad.

The ensuing years of failure broke his health and his heart. He finally had to move in with his sister, and died a miserable death of pneumonia.

Since then, other folks have took up the search for Tobe Inmon's lost silver mine. Treasure hunters have combed the hills up around Moccasin Creek Valley. Some ancient Spanish tools was discovered, and a Cherokee Indian found a large silver nugget in an old mine up there — or so he claimed. He fleeced several hundred dollars from a group of farmers and vanished into the night, never to be seen again. Grover Page found a silver nugget in a cornfield up by Shop Creek. They even say that "ghost lights" dancin' on ridge crests along Moccasin Creek mark the places where pockets of gold and silver ore is located...

Well, sir. All this happened when I was a much younger man. For many years, the story of Tobe Inmon's silver remained a mystery. Finally, over forty years later, I stumbled onto the truth. No other livin' man has ever figgered it out. I am writin' this down now so that the secret won't die with me.

Many years after the events I've related here, radio come into America — and that's what give me the answer! It's plain as the nose on your face, once you think of it. We know that Tobe Inmon went to Texas.

In Laredo, he must have joined up with the Texas Rangers. Later, he took to wearin' a mask, teamed up with a faithful Indian companion (who called him "Kemosabe"), and went gallivantin' all over the West with his silver bullets. You heard it here first, folks. *Tobe Inmon was really the Lone Ranger!*

Yoachum Dollars

Some folks say it all started when the Spanish Conquistadores come to the Ozark Mountains to plunder gold and silver. There was an old cave back in them days that had numerous passageways and a thick vein of silver ore. The first thing the Spaniards did when they got here was to enslave a sizable number of Choctaw Indians to work in the mine. They treated these captives downright nasty, whippin' and starvin' the natives, chainin' them like animals, and workin' them cruel.

The Spaniards built a large log fortress on top of a mountain down near the mouth of the James River, along about where it flows into the White River — mebbe three miles northwest of Lampe, Missouri, near Table Rock Lake. Next thing you know, they excavated tunnels deep into the mountain, followin' the angles and turns of the silver lode. They stored up huge piles of silver ingots ready to ship back to the king in Spain.

Now from time to time, the Spaniards would notice other Choctaw high atop nearby ridges, watchin' how they was treatin' the captive ones. These neighboring Choctaw was growin' hostile and menacin' for some reason. It never occurred to the Spaniards that they was gettin' riled over the way their kinfolk was bein' treated.

So it come as a considerable annoyance to them Spaniards when all the Choctaw in the region gathered together and massacred them to the last man. The silver mine, with all them ingots, remained forgotten for 250 years.

Meanwhile, French trappers and traders come into the region. The Choctaw themselves had little use for silver (except to make ornaments), but they soon found that they could trade the shiny metal for blankets, weapons, horses, and other supplies. So for the next many years, they'd make regular trips to the mine and bring away jist enough ingots to make jewelry and conduct trade. One time a Mexican come to the area with a treasure map lookin' for the Lost Spanish Mine. The Choctaw chief told the Mexican that there was no such mine and they chased him off. The Choctaw closed off the mine and sealed the entrance.

Well, sir. This was at a time when the United States government was movin' Indian tribes around like pawns on a chessboard, with no consideration whatsoever for their feelings. They moved Delawares, Shawnee, Kickapoos, and Senecas into the Ozark Mountains and moved the Choctaw out to Oklahoma for some reason. It made no sense whatsoever — but that's the federal government for you.

About the same time, a feller named James Yoachum moved his family down from Illinois to homestead on the river — which was later named after him. James Yoachum had hunted and trapped in these hills for some years before bringin' down his family, and he'd married a Delaware woman after his first wife died. Joseph Philibert, who run the local trading post, fell in love with Yoachum's pretty young daughter, Peninah Yoachum, and a community feeling began to come about.

James Yoachum continued to hunt and trap, and he planted his bottom land in corn and squash. He bought a handsome herd of cattle and horses. James and his brother Solomon made the best peach brandy in the whole region. They traded furs, meat, and produce at the James Fork Trading Post in exchange for sugar, coffee, flour, fabric, and other staples. Some folks say they also traded liquor to the Indians. James Yoachum soon developed a very productive farm down along the river.

The Delaware Indians was peaceful folks who often brought gifts of food to the new settlers. Because his wife was a Delaware, James Yoachum was considered part of the tribe. He noticed that many of his wife's relatives livin' nearby wore ornaments and jewelry made of high-quality silver — such things as beaded necklaces, arm bands, and hair trinkets. His Delaware friends told him the story of the old cave and the Lost Spanish Mine. James wanted to see the cave, but his in-laws told him that would violate a pact made between the Choctaw and the Delaware never to reveal the location of the silver.

So it was for several years, until the federal government took it into their heads to move all the Delaware out again — this time to Indian Territory in Oklahoma. The Yoachum brothers helped their friends load the wagons and gave them blankets, horses, and cookin' utensils. In return, the Delaware chief told the Yoachums where the Lost Spanish Mine was located. James and Solomon Yoachum vowed never to reveal the secret.

Now the Yoachum brothers had all the silver ingots in the world they could ever want. There was only one problem. *You can't spend ingots any place.* The James Fork Trading Post wouldn't take them, 'cause there was no way to make change. The trading post was operated by a firm named Menard and Valle outta St. Genevieve, Missouri; and they wanted cash. So the Yoachums decided they'd jist make their own coins.

They made up some dies, melted down the silver ingots, rolled the pure silver into sheets, and stamped out their own dollars. Their coins was a might larger than the regular United States issue, and they had "Yoachum" stamped onto one side and "1822" on t'other.

Since they was larger than a U.S. dollar and had higher silver content, folks was more than happy to accept Yoachum dollars. Over a period of months, the Yoachum brothers minted thousands of these coins and put them into circulation all through the mountains. In later years, one old-timer recalled that, as a boy, he'd seen a large barrel in the Yoachum barn filled right near to the brim with Yoachum dollars. They come to be more common than United States money.

Now that the Delaware Indians was gone, the federal government decided to open up the former Indian lands for settlement. A land office was set up in Springfield for folks to register their new land claims. And settlers who'd owned their homesteads for years was told they also had to file for title to the property they lived on. They was all required to pay filing fees to the government.

Folks from all over Missouri come to the government office to file their claims and pay their fees. One day, several dozen mountaineers showed up in Springfield to purchase some of the newly available Indian land. The men was hot and tired from their long journey from the James River area, but they lined up at the land office peacefully.

The little government agent on duty, however, refused to accept Yoachum dollars. He got out his rules and regulations book and cited a legislation from 1833 requirin' that all such payments be made in federal-issue coins. He then looked up from his rule book to find hisself surrounded by hostile mountain men pointin' loaded shotguns at his head.

"These here Yoachum dollars are what us folks use hereabouts, young feller. Yoachum dollars mean more to us-uns than enny of yer dern government money. If you-uns know what's good for ye, take these here Yoachum dollars ... or suffer the consequences."

The government agent suddenly remembered an even older book of his, which advised: *when in Rome, do as the Romans do.* He accepted the Yoachum dollars and presented each man with a valid title certificate for his land. But, bein' a dedicated public servant and loyal government employee, he wrote a detailed report and sent it back to Washington, D.C., along with the dollars.

Some early newspaper reports refer to Yoachum dollars as coun‐
terfeit, but the federal authorities did not consider them so.
There was no attempt to duplicate U.S. government-minted
coins — they was all clearly marked "Yoachum". Nor could they
be considered fraudulent, because when they was assayed, the
coins was found to be almost pure silver. They contained much
more silver than was found in government-issued dollars. The
government agent in Springfield was ordered to confiscate the
Yoachum dollars and to determine the location of the silver mine.

Well, sir. The loyal government agent eventually did locate
the Yoachum farm. But when he asked to see the silver mine,
James Yoachum ordered the feller off his property — at gun‐
point. So of course, the federal government sent a whole army
of agents down with plenty of guns to show James Yoachum
the error of his ways.

James was convinced.

"Why, do you-uns mean to say that I bin breakin' the laws of
the Yew-Nighted States of Amerika? Wal, I shore never know'd
thet. I'm a patriot — I never willingly broke the law in mah life."

So James Yoachum agreed to stop mintin' coins. But he refused to tell the federal government where his silver mine was located. James and his brother Solomon kept that secret till the end of their days.

Now what you have jist heard is one version of the story of the Yoachum dollars. There are others. Some folk think it's jist another Ozark tall tale, as full of moonshine as a starry mountain night. But the fact remains that this story is true. Several coin collectors around the nation still have Yoachum dollars in their possession to this very day. And on March 11, 1983, a feller by the name of J.R. Blunk from Galena, Missouri, was diggin' near a riverbank on some property by the old Yoachum homestead, when he found a big clump of hard wax. He broke it open — and inside was the original iron dies used to stamp out the Yoachum dollars!

Some folks say the Lost Spanish Mine never existed. They claim that James and Solomon Yoachum got their silver by illegally sellin' liquor to the Delaware Indians in exchange for U.S. dollars, which they then melted them down so they couldn't be traced. They say the Yoachum brothers jist made up the story of the Lost Mine to cover their outlaw activities.

Now I never heard of such a dern-fool notion. Wherever the Yoachum brothers got their silver, it warn't from meltin' down United States coinage. If the Yoachum dollars was made by meltin' US dollars — *how could they have a much higher silver content than the coins they was made from?*

It's still a mystery to this day.

The Vanishing Island

At a certain camp near Branson, Missouri, the guides used to tell about a mysterious island that would sometimes appear out of the mists on Lake Taneycomo jist after a mountain thunderstorm. At such times, there would be strange waves rippling on the water and crashing onto rocks along the shoreline. Every few minutes or so, the water level of the lake would rise about four feet and then recede again. By the time anyone could get to their boats to investigate, the island would have vanished.

Finally, a stalwart group of boatmen managed to get launched and make their way through the choppy waters slapping against their boat to land on the island, the surface of which was smooth, slippery rocks with algae growing in the wet crevices. The whole island seemed to rise and fall, and there was a sound like steam escaping from a blow hole somewhere. One of the men made his way up to the highest part of the hill, from where he could see the entire island. The feller became wildly excited, waving his hat and shouting as he scarpered back down the slope and ran for the boat.

"Row for your lives, boys!!" he shouted as he dove into the boat and readied the oars. "This ain't no island! It's the biggest gaw-daffle snapping turtle in the world!"

And so it was. They had been standing on its shell. Every time the monster breathed, the waters rose and fell. But no one was surprised, really — turtles grow mighty large in the Ozarks. One big snapper down in the Buffalo River swallowed a mule that was swimming across, and when the monster was shot four years later, the horseshoes was found still in its stomach. Even mosquitoes down here can grow big enough to carry off a blue-tick hound.

The Yankee and the Vampire

There was once two Yankee soldiers captured by the Confederate Army and taken to a prisoner camp in Missouri. Now one of these Yankees was a short, swarthy feller with a wart on his nose. He had once lived in Missouri as a child, and knew his way around the Ozarks. The other soldier was a tall, gangly lad from Illinois; he was awkward and bony and looked for all the world like Abraham Lincoln's homelier cousin.

Now the Rebel boys that was guardin' the camp found out that the tall soldier would believe everything he was told, so they filled his head with ghost stories and tales of Ozark monsters.

Well, sir. There wasn't much goin' on in that part of the war, so things was kinda laid-back in the prisoner of war camp. The short soldier (they called him "Warty"), he got tiresome bored with bein' a prisoner; and the tall soldier (he was called "Lank") got homesick for his mother's cooking. So they decided to have an escape.

They had no trouble gettin' out of camp — the guards was all pretty lax. But then they had quite a number of miles to go to reach Illinois, and much of it was through the Ozark mountains. Warty felt right at home, and enjoy hikin' through the backwoods scenery. But poor Lank saw bears behind every bush and monsters in every cave.

Of course they had no gear and had to sleep in the rough, but it was springtime and things warn't as bad as camp life had been in the Yankee army. One day, Lank and Warty come on an abandoned cabin up on Hookram's Mountain. It had cracked

boards and broken windows, rags for curtains, and mold growin' on the walls. The place looked like something out of one of them stories by Edgar Allan Poe.

Warty was delighted. "We'll sleep in a soft old bed tonight, Lank!" he declared.

But the tall soldier wasn't so sure. "Looks to me like there'd be ghosts in that place — or something worse."

"Nonsense," said Warty as he opened the cabin door and walked in.

The inside was even more scary-lookin' than the outside had been. Lank timidly peered into the cabin, holdin' onto the doorframe in case he needed to push off for a hasty exit. Warty found some old dried beans in the cupboard and managed to cook them in the fireplace, usin' a dented and cracked bucket to boil them in. After this meager repast, Warty was happy and contented. He stretched out in an old chair with his feet up on the bucket and began playin' his mouth harp.

"Ain't you afraid the Rebels will hear you?" said Lank, peerin' out the window into the darkness.

"No fear of that," Warty said. "There ain't nothing human this side of Hookram's Mountain." That didn't comfort Lank none.

Lank sat down on the floor with his back to the wall and his long, bony legs drawn up under his chin. He was tremblin' so bad that his knobby knees knocked together. The tall soldier nearly jumped out of his skin when an old hoot owl whistled outside the window. Finally, the two soldiers turned in to sleep in the creakin' old bed.

"I'm jist sure there must be ghosts or goblins or boogeymen in this place!" said Lank.

"Oh, shut up and go to sleep," said the short soldier.

Warty was asleep in no time, but Lank didn't sleep a wink all night. Every time the wind rustled the rag curtains or a mouse scratched somewheres, the tall soldier nearly died of fright. Then the wind died down and the moon went behind dark clouds.

The mountain become dreadawfulsome quiet, the room was blacker than pitch, and the smell of mold hung in the air. Then — faintly — Lank heard an eerie sound. It was a high-pitched keening, like the cry of a lost soul. And it was comin' closer....

The sound got louder and louder. Then Lank felt a whiff of air brush his face *even though the wind was dead still.* The sound was close now, terrible loud in his ears. Then, something with six long fingers stretched out and grabbed his neck!

Lank screamed like a baby with a thorn in its diapers. He grabbed at his neck and felt something big, horrible-soft, and squishy; then his whole hand was covered with drippin' warm blood. Warty woke up jist as the moon come out again. He looked at his companion in disgust.

"What's the matter with you, boy?" Warty said. "Ain't you never slapped a mosquito before?"

They do grow mosquitoes powerful big down here.

Jesse James' Final Escape

Now Jesse and Frank James was known for evadin' the law. Most every cave in the Ozarks was said to have been used by the notorious outlaws at one time or t'other as a hideout. They had more tricks up their sleeves than a blue-tick hound has fleas.

Jesse used to write letters to the newspapers, paintin' hisself as a war hero and Robin Hood of the Old South — helpin' poor folks and fightin' the Yankees. "I have lived as a peaceable citizen, and obeyed the laws of the United States to the best of my knowledge," he wrote to the *Kansas City Times*. The general public was not aware that the James brothers was the leaders of an outlaw gang until four years afterwards.

The James boys won the support of folks in the countryside; they seem to stand for the lost Confederacy — gallant, chivalrous, and defiant. When they robbed banks, folks wished them well. This made things a might difficult for the Pinkerton detectives, who was always hot on their trails. The Pinkertons was, after all — Yankees. And they got precious little help from Missouri folk in tryin' to catch the outlaws.

Jesse was always one to look out for his own hide, even at the expense of the rest of his gang. Jist lookit how he and Frank skedaddled out of Minnesota after robbin' the bank at Northfield — leavin' Cole Younger and his brothers behind to get captured.

Things went downhill for Frank and Jesse after the Northfield fiasco. They'd been used to robbin' banks in Missouri, where folks was kinda laid-back and easygoing. Them crazy Norwegians in Minnesota surprised the gang — their ancestors was Vikings, an' they was a might less tolerant of bein' robbed than folks back home was, and a whole lot tougher in a fight.

Jesse tried to recruit a new gang, and he managed to rob three more trains; but the James Gang's heyday was over. Their main achievement in later years was in avoidin' arrest. They remained at large year after year, and still possessed a certain flamboyant style. But, nevertheless, it was time to retire.

The problem was that the Pinkerton agents would never let Frank and Jesse live in peace. When Jesse first come back from Minnesota with a bullet in his leg, he had dinner with his doctor at Fulton's Whaley Hotel in Kansas City — where they shared a table with several Pinkerton agents who had come to Missouri to hunt for Jesse James. He once ran into D.G. Bligh in Kentucky. Bligh was the first detective ever assigned to hunt the James Gang many years before, and Jesse had a nice visit with him. Jesse later sent the unsuspectin' detective a postcard, informin' him that he'd finally met up with Jesse James at last.

But the governor of Missouri was offerin' a sizable reward for the James boys, and Jesse know'd that it was only a matter of time before the Pinkertons got him. So he come up with a ruse to get them off his back forever.

There was another outlaw in the Ozark hills who'd been a thorn in Jesse's side for years. Charlie Bigelow had robbed banks back in the 1880s, usin' the alias of "Jesse James" to avoid the law. He even looked a tad like Jesse. Then there was a neighboring farmer near the James place by the name of Sam Collins, who'd been foolin' around with Frank's wife, Annie, while the gang was on the trail.

Frank made a deal with Sam Collins whereby, for $25,000 and title to the James farm, Sam would impersonate Frank James for the rest of his life — and have Annie as his wife.

The gang found Charlie Bigelow and shot him. They brought his body to Jesse James' house in St. Joseph, Missouri, and laid him out on the floor under a crooked picture on the wall. Bob Ford shot his pistol into the wall and then ran out to collect the reward for havin' killed Jesse James.

Frank arranged for hisself to get pardoned by the governor, turned his life and wife over to Sam Collins, and moved to Arkansas under the name Joe Vaughn. He built a cabin on the Buffalo River, married a neighbor's daughter, and raised nine children. Jesse traveled to South America, Texas, and Oklahoma under the alias J.F. Dalton, and lived to be over 100 years old.

Frank James told his family his true identity while on his deathbed in 1926, and gave them a manuscript that told the whole story of the hoax. The family remembered Jesse visitin' their home as late as 1920, but they never know'd who he was until 1948 when they saw Jesse's photograph in the paper.

In that year, the 100-year-old Jesse James came forward in Lawton, Oklahoma, and revealed his identity. He traveled home to Missouri, where he was examined and questioned intensively. His physical characteristics, wounds, and scars was identical to those of the notorious outlaw. Old men who had known Jesse in the old days was brought to Missouri, where they all identified J.F. Dalton as the man they'd known as the leader of the James Gang.

So in the end, ol' Jesse James outwitted the Pinkertons, got revenge on his enemies, and outlived them all — at least so the story goes.

Ozark Eddie Tales

Ozark Eddie is undoubtedly the kind-heartedest human being I ever met. A great bear of a man with lantern jaw, dressed in bib overalls with a wide mountaineer's hat and Kentucky rifle, Ozark Eddie is the fundamental mountain man. He roams the woods and swamps around Bootlegger's Mountain, keeping an eye on the homes of neighbors while they're away, taking care of elderly ladies living alone, and maintaining a pet graveyard in the woods for dogs that die in the neighborhood.

He wears a pair of handcuffs on a rope tied around his waist — in case he catches chicken thieves. (Eddie once caught a miscreant stealing some of his ol' Daddy's hens, run him down, sat on him, and kept him cuffed till the Sheriff arrived.) He wears a heavy chain around his neck with two cowbells, for the benefit of neighbors who don't have doorbells. There is no mistaking when Ozark Eddie comes to call. He stands in the yard clanking the bell and hollering "Eddie! Eddie!"

His ol' daddy was a slender little man who looked like a gnome next to his massive son. But Daddy had big hands and wore a size 15 ring. They lived in a house he'd put together out of various things, but it was a good home and he raised a fine family in it.

Eddie is the genuine article. A true Ozark mountaineer living the simple life of earlier generations. The police like Eddie because he is strictly honest, and knows everyone and everything that goes on in the hills. Whenever local rascals are up to mischief, Eddie can tell you who was responsible for the latest housebreaking, petty thieving, or other outrage.

Ozark Eddie is a marvelous (if somewhat modest) storyteller, relating his personal adventures in a mountain dialect so thick you could cut it with a chainsaw.

Oh-hoe. Okay, you was talkin' about that haunted house down there. The old haunted house that was tore down. They tore that sucker down.

I was sittin' on the porch restin' when I was walkin' home one night. I got tired an' that; I jist went up there an' set down. Whatever it was that was in the house, I quieten 'em down. I think it mighta been somebody in there makin' whiskey, I don't know. I banged on the wall one time. After I went O-WHOOM — that was it. I quieten 'em down an' didn't stick around.

I used to go down there all the time. Take some Vienna sausages down there an' eat an' be left alone. The guy that owns the place used to let me go huntin' an' fishin' on that property. He wouldn't let nobody else go on the property, but he let me.

One night, I'd had a bad day an' my back was hurtin'. I jist wanted to be left alone, you know, an' not be bothered by nobody. So I went down there in the back of that house an' was sleepin' down there when I heard this racket. These guys was comin' in an' woke me up. It jist scared me half to death.

Some kids, maybe a girlfriend an' boyfriend, probably, were checkin' out the house to mess around. I don't know who it was — it might of been those Duffel kids, I don't know.

I went *"Hoooo-oo!"*— an' they took off out of the building runnin' like they'd seen a ghost or something, you know? Since then, I haven't seen them again. They thought the place was haunted when they saw me in there.

About a month or a year later after that experience happened, a tornado come down here an' jist about to blowed us away. It jumped across the lake an' wiped out about three or four houses. I seen it jump right over the roof of my house. Brother, it scared me half to death. There was a guy down here name of — I can't think of his name — it tore right over the top of his house, too, an' jist kept on going.

I had to walk around the lake all night to keep the thieves from lootin' stuff. Finally, the Law came out here an' they put up roadblocks and everything; it took 'em several hours to get people out here to do it. I went on home. I couldn't go to sleep; I was just so nervous an' upset about the tornado an' everything.

I couldn't go to sleep. So I went down out to Vicki's to see if they needed any help. I was walkin' down the road an' the Law threatened to arrest me if I didn't go home. So I said, "Man, I can't sleep. There's no way, either — I tried, I went for five days, an' I still can't go to sleep."

I told 'em, "I have a bottle of whiskey, but I'm not drunk. I'm jist so upset about it."

The Law say, "Okay, if you want to help, we'll give you a flashlight an' put you down on the road somewhere. You ain't supposed to be out here. But we'll deputize you or something, you know."

They had to let me — I was bein' such a pain in the neck. How would you feel if you came close to gettin' your house blown away?

I'd of been happy to sleep all night.

Okay, the governor came out here — I can't remember who the governor was then — but he came out here an' I shook hands with the governor. The helicopters landed over by where that big fancy swimmin' pool in town is. We met the National Guard an' all that stuff. I think it took us a long time to clean this place up. But we finally cleaned it up.

I was a local deputy for a while, till they got all that place cleaned up. Like a night watchman for a while. I was kind of like in charge of walkin' around an' makin' sure that, you know, they was doin' their job an' stuff. That's all I done.

My grandpa was deputy sheriff in Coal Valley, Alabama, before he died, an' he still had his papers when he come down here. The old sheriff — not the new one — made him a kind of temporary deputy. My grandpa couldn't see too good; he had only one good eye. We'd jist walk around sometimes at night. But he got so sick that he finally died, of coal miner's disease.

I do walk around quite a bit an' visit with the neighbors when I don't got anythin' else to do. Come down here an' check on your mother to make sure I don't find her dead. I did find somebody dead the other day. They'd had a heart attack. Old Man Duffel went up there an' banged on the door an' nobody came to the door. We got the state police an' the sheriff's department to come out here.

There's always somebody dyin' or gettin' shot or run off the road, an' all that stuff. There used to be bootleggers here a long, long time ago — but not any more. Joe Dunbar used to have a black man to make whiskey. They found his still shot full of bullet holes an' threw it into the lake, an' that's where it stayed at. All the fish used to get drunk an' you'd see them floatin' up on top of the water.

When my grandpa was alive, they used to make whiskey an' take it out there an' store it in wood kegs an' put it in the creek to keep it cool. It was pretty good whiskey; I drank some of it.

Joe was a bootlegger. He was the one who made the whiskey. There were people up there makin' whiskey an' stuff. I hardly heard of any of them. But the only experience I ever heard my daddy talk about, he said he was up around Toad Suck or somewhere — some little bitty town. He an' my grandpa was hunting. Somebody was out there makin' whiskey, an' that man say, "Don't you come any closer." Somethin' like that. They were makin' whiskey out there, 'cause Daddy told me so; he could smell it.

When these guys moved down here, there was only two houses. All mud roads. My grandma had a great big old Dodge car, an' it got stuck down in the middle of the road right around this corner down here. It took us an' two tractors an' two mules to get that sucker out. It was buried all the way down to the axle; I had to get a shovel to dig it out.

Chicken thieves? *Owww,* I don't want to talk about that. We rasseled down in the mud an' everything. That was pitiful. I lost the key to the handcuffs an' had to get a hacksaw to cut 'em off. That was a terrible experience.

Well, it jist happened to be one night my daddy an' them weren't home an' it was pourin' down raining. I heard the chickens makin' all kinds of racket — screamin' an' hollering, you know. I thought it was a fox out there. I went to get my shotgun an' seen a guy walkin' the road with this big old bag of chickens, you know.

"Hey, stop you stupid jerk!" A-heh. I ran after him, you know, cacklin' an' chickens goin' everywhere. I don't want to talk about that experience. I handcuffded him. I jist walked him around handcuffded all night. I took him into the house an' dialed the operator an' said, "I need an emergency. Git the sheriff's department out here."

They said they'd come on out. I locked him up to the fence post till they got out there an' got a hacksaw an' took 'em off. They took him in to jail an' kept him there for about three or four days an' made him pay for the chickens.

But I tell you what, I've had some crazy experiences.

I think the craziest experience I ever had, I went squirrel huntin' one time. I shot this squirrel that was in a tree — an' I couldn't get it out. So I went down an' got another guy, an' he shot it again an' blew it out of the tree. He was a better shot than I was. I went home an' cooked it, you know.

I'll tell you a crazy experience that happened, an' this is true — you guys will laugh about this. Greg Ryan an' some boys down here had a 'possum up in our tree, an' they wanted to snare it an' sell it. But my daddy wouldn't come out there an' cut the tree down, so they were goin' to try to smoke the 'possum out.

They caught the whole tree on fire. I was throwin' dirt up there, tryin' to put it out. Had to call in the whole neighborhood to put it out. They had to cut the tree down to put it out — an' like to burn the whole woods down. It jist barbecued those 'possums; there was nothin' left of 'em. An' that's the truth. I got people up there can tell you about that.

That big fish? Oh, yeah, my daddy caught that out here on a trout line, me an' him did. We like to drowned ourself pullin' that thing in the boat. We didn't have that big ol' boat my daddy's got now — that great big iron boat got foam an' everything in it. We had that little bitty aluminum boat, an' we like to tip that aluminum boat over tryin' to get that fish in there. We got the net up there, an' like to rip the net all to pieces 'cause it was an old net, you know. *Whew!* I forgot how much that fish weighed. I think it was close to 50 pounds, I don't know. I don't really remember now. It was a big fish — all I know. I caught some buffalo out there you couldn't put your arms around, like this. Buffalo fish...

A buffalo is a fish — what you think I'm talkin' about, you bean-head? Real buffalo? Well, I had an experience with those, too.

When we had the mud roads out here, the Brama cows got loose an' came up in my yard an' knocked over my garbage cans an' sat down in the middle of the yard an' started eatin' grass. I run them out of the yard. I got a bunch of firecrackers to throw at it an' run it off. We found out later on that it was Major Lewis' cows.

Okay, there was some guys that had some real, live buffalo. An' they got loose. One was sittin' right out in the middle of the road, an' wouldn't even get out of the road. He was out there stoppin' traffic — they had about ten cars stopped up there at the end of the road. They jist couldn't run over him, you know, it would have dented somebody's car.

I was down there, stuck in the road. I had to do something. I had no choice. I got up an' beat at that thing an' said, "Git, you — get off the road or *I will make you* get off the road!" I tried to grab him by the neck, you know, an' pull him an' choke him — but he jist sit there.

He finally got up an' 'bout to kill me right there at the fence.

The Hand of God

You know, men have seen queer sights in these Ozark Mountains, especially when the weather hangs like a shroud over the rocky ridges and tree-covered slopes. There are times when the fog fills the Taneycomo Valley right up to the brim, and a man standing on the top of the ridge can see clear sky overhead and a witches' cauldron of thick, stirring mist below. There are times when thunderstorms shake the hillsides and rain comes down hard; the boulders and rocks get so slickery that if lightning strikes a ridge, it bounces right off again and ricochets three or five times down the canyon walls. On such occasions, the road pavement is even slicker than the rocks, and no sane man would drive those hairpin turns and switchbacks along the ridge roads at a speed faster than 3.2 miles per hour.

Of course, that don't keep the good ol' mountain boys from roaring along those Ozark roads in the rain with their foot to the pedal and goin' like lickety-thunder themselves. They make it three or eight miles or so before sailin' off a cliff; and then — if they ain't kilt — they have to sit there and wait for a wrecker truck or some farmer with a tractor and log chain to come along and pull 'em back up so's they can take off again.

It was during jist such a rainstorm that my Uncle Lemuel got religion.

The boys up on Rumpus Ridge in those days was a fun-lovin' if somewhat rowdy bunch. On Friday and Saturday nights, they'd all wind up down at the Bingbuffer Tavern where fat, jovial P.T. McQuary and young Jim O'Grady would serve up moonshine and mountain dew as fast as the good ol' boys could guzzle it down.

My Uncle Lem lived on the other side of Hookrum's Mountain clear past 'Possum Hollow and way beyond. There was a fair bit o' mountain road between his shack and Rumpus Ridge; you had to walk up the trail to the top of the mountain and down t'other side, clear past Piney Ridge, and then follow the blacktop thru the woods and down along Dead Man's Drop till you came to Lucan McCann's cabin, then left eight or ten miles to Rumpus Ridge.

Now on that particular night it was rainin' paynters and coons, with wind and lightning and thunder roaring like cannons. There was times the rain fell so hard thet Uncle Lem could't see the corn cob on the end of his pipe-stem. He were a dour ol' man, and he didn't mind walkin' forty miles to get a drink. But this night was a bit much even for him. So he slid down the muddy slope to the blacktop and decided to hitch a ride to the Bingbuffer Tavern.

Wal, as you might imagine, there warn't much traffic on the road that night. Fact be told, Uncle Lem trudged along the blacktop for two hours without seein' nary a vehicle. But at last, when he was jist about done for, a car glided up out of the drivin' rain and rolled to a stop beside him. Never hesitatin' a moment, Uncle Lem opened the passenger door and clambered inside.

The car lurched forward into the stormy night with rain poundin' on the windshield like fury. It warn't till a big flash o' lightning that Uncle Lem realized *there warn't nobody at the wheel...*

Uncle Lem was alone in the car!

He was afraid to reach out and feel the empty space behind the steerin' wheel to see if maybe an invisible man or a haint was sittin' there. The car crested a rise and began acceleratin' downslope.

The winding road was following the edge of a sheer bluff that fell the better part of a mile straight down. Up ahead was the dreadawfulsome hairpin curve at Dead Man's Drop, and the car was headed straight for the cliff. Uncle Lem pictured himself dashed to bits on the jagged rocks below. He was so terrified he couldn't move.

Now up to this time, Uncle Lem had not been much of a religious man. But current circumstances seemed to be calling for a change in his attitude. He began prayin' like he'd never prayed before. "Oh Dear God, *pleeese* don't let this car go a-plungin' off that awful cliff!!"

But the car kept pickin' up speed.

Then — at the last possible second — an enormous hand materialized in thru the open driver's window, seized the steering wheel, and pulled it to the left. The car swerved around the switchback and kept on rushin' down the mountainside road. The enormous hand vanished away into the rain and mist as mysterious as it had come.

But there were alot more cliffs and curves between Dead Man's Drop and Rumpus Ridge. Uncle Lem kept on a-prayin' for his life, and each time the enormous hand would appear at the last moment and turn the steerin' wheel. Uncle Lem's heart was thumpin' like a trip-hammer, and it had a disconcertin' habit of leapin' up into his throat from time to time. Then at last, when the hainted car was a few hundred yards from Rumpus Ridge, Uncle Lem flung open the door and scrambled out of that car as fast as he could travel — headin' straight for the Bingbuffer Tavern.

Uncle Lemule was wild-haired an' soaking wet; and his eyes was bulging the way hardboiled eggs pop from their shells when they been overcooked. He was ravin' about Dead Man's Drop and the Hand of God and such-like, and those good ol' boys all thought he's been hittin' the moonshine crock pretty hard. But as he sat gaspin' and sobbin' on a stool at the bar and related his tale, they slowly realized that Uncle Lem was stone-cold sober. The room grew silent as those rugged mountain men pondered his eerie tale.

It warn't till about a half-hour later that the tavern door opened and Ozark Eddie walked in with his ol' Daddy. Eddie took one look at Uncle Lem, then turned to his father and said: "*Woh-hoe* — lookit there, daddy!! That's the same crazy guy that climbed into yore car when we were pushin' it home in the rain."

The Buffalo That Climbed a Tree

Y'know, when Mark Twain was a young man, he went west —
to the great silverland of the Nevada Territory, by way of the
Overland Stage. And Mark Twain used to tell a tale about one
of the other passengers they had on that stagecoach trip, back
in the year 1860-somethin'-or-other.

He said: Mr. George Bemis was our fellow traveller. He
was a stranger; we had never seen him before. He wore in his
belt an old original Allen Revolver, which folks used to call
a Pepperbox. It had six barrels. Simply drawing the trigger back
cocked and fired this
formidable weapon.

As the trigger came
back, the hammer
begun to rise and
the barrels to turn
over. Down would
come the hammer
and away would fly
the ball. Now it was a difficult thing to *aim* along them turn-
ing barrels. And hitting what was aimed at is a feat which was
probably never achieved with an Allen Pepperbox.

But it was a reliable weapon nevertheless. Because, as one of
the stage drivers said, "If she didn't hit what she was aimed at,
why, she'd hit something else instead!" And so she did.

Bemis once fired at a Jack of Spades that was nailed to a tree...
and hit a *mule* that was standing some thirty yards off to the

left. Now Bemis did not want the mule. But the mule's owner came out with a double-barreled shotgun and persuaded him to buy it anyhow.

Ah, it was a cheerful weapon, the Allen! Sometimes all six barrels would go off at once, and then there warn't no safe place in the whole county — except behind it!

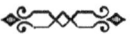

We came at last to the shallow, yellow, muddy South Platte River, with its low banks and scattering of flat sandbars and islands. A melancholy stream straggling through an enormous flat plain.

Next morning, jist before dawn, we were some 500 miles out from St. Josephs, Missouri, when our stagecoach broke down. We was to be delayed for a matter of five or six hours, so we took up an invitation to join a buffalo hunt.

Ah, it was noble sport, gallopin' across the prairie in the dewy freshness of the morning! But our part of the hunt ended in disaster and disgrace. For a wounded buffalo bull chased passenger Bemis nearly two miles, where he abandoned his horse and took to a lone tree.

Bemis was sullen about this matter for some 24 hours. But at last he began to come around a little, and finally he said, "Well, sir, it warn't funny. There was no sense in those cowboys making the remarks they did about me. I tell you, I was angry in earnest, for a while. I would have shot that feller they called Hank, if I could have done it without crippling five or six other people. But of course I couldn't. The Allen is so confounded comprehensive.

"I wish those loafers had been up there in that tree with me; they wouldn't have laughed. If I'd have had a horse worth two cents, but NOOOooo! The minute he saw that buffalo bull wheel on him and bellow, why he raised straight up in the air and stood on his heels — *and danced!* The saddle began to slip, so I took hold of him around the neck and hung on.

"Then down he come and stood on the other end for a while. That buffalo actually stopped pawin' and bellowin' to contemplate this spectacle.

"Then the bull come at me. It was so close, it seemed to literally prostrate my horse's sense of reason, and make a ravin' distracted maniac out of him. *And I hope I may die* if he didn't stand on his head for a quarter of a minute and shed tears!

"That horse was absolutely out of his mind. He was! As sure as Truth itself, he was. And he really didn't know what he was a-doin'.

"Then that buffalo come chargin' at us. And my horse took off! For the next ten minutes, *he actually turned handsprings,* one after another, so fast that the buffalo began to get unsettled, too. He didn't know quite what to do, so he jist stood there sneezin', bellerin' every now and then, and thinking he'd got hisself a $1500 circus horse for breakfast.

"I was first out on the horse's neck, then underneath, next back on his rump; sometimes head up and sometimes heels — but I tell you! I tell you it was solumn *awful,* to be rippin' and tearin' and carryin' on like that in the presence of Death.

"Pretty soon the buffalo made a snatch for us — and come away with a piece of my horse's tail. And then you should have seen that spider-legged old skeleton go! And you ought to have seen the buffalo cut out after him, too; head down, tongue out, tail up, and bellowin' like everything. Actually MOWING DOWN THE WEEDS, tearin' up the earth, and boostin' up sand like a whirlwind.

"By George, it was a hot race! I was sittin' in the saddle on the horse's rump, I had the bridle in my teeth and was holdin' on to the pommel with both hands.

"First, we left the dogs behind. Then we passed a jackrabbit; then we overtook a coyote. We was a-gainin' on an antelope when the rotten saddle let loose and threw me about thirty yards off to the left. As the saddle slid down over the horse's rump, he gave a kick that sent it over 400 yards straight up in the air. I wish I may die in a minute if he didn't!

"I fell at the foot of the only tree that was around for nine counties. And the very next second I had ahold of that tree with four sets of nails and my teeth! And the second after that, I was a-straddle the main limb forty feet up, and blasphemin' my luck in a way that made my breath smell of brimstone.

"Well, sir, I was safe now. I was safe now as long as that buffalo didn't think of one thing. But it was that one thing I dreaded. I dreaded it seriously. There was a possibility that the buffalo might not think of it. But there was a greater chance that he would. So I made up my mind I'd be ready for him!

"I cautiously unwound the lariat from the pommel of my saddle..."

— *"Your saddle? Did you take your saddle up in the tree with you?"*

"Take it up in the tree with me? Of course I didn't! No man coulda done that. It fell in the tree when it come down."

— *"What?!!"*

"Are you doubtin' my word?"

— *"No, no, I wouldn't do that..."*

"Well, sir. I unwound the lariat. I fastened one end of it to the limb. I made a slip-noose in the other end, and hung it down to see how far it went. It reached half-way to the ground. I then loaded every barrel of the Allen with a double charge, and I was satisfied. I said, 'As long as that buffalo never thinks of that one thing, I'll be all right. And even if he does, I'm fixed for him!'

"But friends, don't you know that the very thing — THE VERY THING a man dreads most, well, that's the thing that always happens. Indeed it's so! I watched that buffalo with anxiety. Anxiety of which no man can conceive who's not been in such a situation, when sudden death might come at any minute.

"And presently, a thought came into that buffalo's eye. I knew it! *I knew it!* I said: 'If my nerve fails me now, I'm lost!' Sure enough, it was the very thing I had dreaded. The buffalo ... BEGAN TO CLIMB THE TREE!"

— *"WHAT?!"*

"You heard me."

— *"But, but ... buffalo's can't climb trees!"*

"Who says they can't? Have you ever seen one try?"

— *"No, of course not!"*

"Well, then, you jist keep quiet! Jist 'cause YOU'VE never seen a thing don't mean it can't happen!"

— *"All right, all right, go on! What'd you do?"*

"Well, sir. The buffalo started up. And he got about ten feet up — and then he slipped! And he slid back. I breathed easier. But then he tried it again, he got up a little higher, slipped, but then he come on and this time he was more careful.

"Gradually, he climbed higher and higher. And as he did, my my spirits went down more and more. Up and up he came. An inch at a time, with his eyes hot and his tongue hangin' out. Higher and higher. He hooked his hoof over the stump of a limb and looked up at me, as much as if to say, 'You're my meat, friend!'

"Up higher and higher, and gettin' more excited the closer he got. He was within ten feet of me. I took a deep breath. It was now or never!

"I had the coil with the lariat all ready. I played it out slowly till I had it hung right over his head. And then I let go of the slack, and the slipnoose fell right 'round his neck. Quicker than lightnin', I whipped out the Allen and I let him have it with all six barrels — point blank — right in the face. *BLAMMM!*

"It must have scared that buffalo right out of his senses.

"Well, sir. When that smoke cleared away, there he was — danglin' in the air twenty feet off the ground, and going into convulsions. Well, sir. I shinnied down that tree and headed straight for home as fast as I could."

— *"Bemis, is this all true, jist as you've stated it?"*

"I hope to rot in my tracks and die if it ain't!"

— *"Well, it's not that we don't believe you. But perhaps if there was some proof..."*

"PROOF? You want PROOF? Did I bring back my lariat?"

— "No."

"Did I bring back my horse?"

— "No."

"Did any of you ever see that buffalo again?"

— *"No..."*

"Well, sir, then what more do you want? I never saw anybody as particular as *you* about a little thing like proof!"

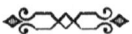

I made up my mind that if this man Bemis wasn't a liar, he only missed it *by the skin of his teeth!*

How the First Rat Come to Missouri

Now back in the real old days, there was a feller named Noah built hisself a big boat, an ark, 'cause God said he was goin' ta make it rain for a spell. An' it rained for forty days and forty nights. Now Noah was the first animal rights activist, an' he was concerned with endangered species. So he took two of every animal on the ark with him, ta save them from the flood. An' he took a male an' a female of each critter.

Now there were two exceptions to that. The first was human bein's. There was a lot more than two, 'cause Noah took his wife an' chilluns an' all his kinfolk with him. An' the other exception was the Norway Rat — 'cause of course, rats always go on ships an' ya can't keep 'em off. He had a lot o' rats.

So here Noah was on the Ark with his kinfolk and a whole boatload of critters and a few dozen rats. An' they sailed all over the world lookin' for a place to land. Of course, they couldn't find nowheres, 'cause the whole place was drownded.

'Cept, of course, for northern Arkansas an' Missouri.

Now that part of the world is used to dreadawfulsome weather. Down there they got snappin' turtles so big that folks think they're islands — an' mosquitos in Missouri grow so bodacious huge they get mistook for vampire bats. _WHY_ — forty days and forty nights o' rain down thar warn't nothin'. It was second thing on to a drowt.

So when Noah and his kinfolk finally spied land, it were a mountain in the area now known as Branson, Missouri. An' when they come up thar and threw out the anchor, there was a hillbilly an' his wife a-sittin' there under a tree lookin' up at the boat. Now Noah's wife was fixin' to unload all the critters, but before she was ready, one of them thar Norway Rats hopped up an' started climbin' down the anchor chain.

Now until that day, there hadn't been no rats in Arkansas or Missouri — an' the hillybilly's wife had never seen such a varmint. So just as Noah leaned over the rail and hollered, "*Oi* — what place is this we've landed? What's the name of that mountain?" At the very same moment, the hillybilly's wife noticed the rat climbin' down the anchor chain, an' she said, "Say, Lemuel, what kinda critter aer thet a-climbin' down the anchor chain?"

An' Lem said: "That aer a rat."

So naturally Noah thought the feller was answerin' him, an' that the mountain was named 'Aer-A-Rat'. It was all the more confusin' because there really is a mountain with a similar name in another part of the world. So Noah wrote down in the ship's log that they had landed at Mount Ararat.

But truth be told, Noah's Ark actually landed there at what today is known as Branson, Missouri.

An' there is scientific confirmation and proof of the fact, too. 'Cause after the water subsided an' Noah an' his kinfolk lit out for other territories, they left behind the big boat. It become quite an attraction down thar. None of them hillbillies had ever seen such a big thang. Folks come from all over ta see Noah's Ark. An' pretty soon, that whole dern area become known as the N'ozark Mountains. An' it's known by that name to this very day.

About the Author

Alan Lance Andersen is president and director of PALLADIAN Interactive Theatre, LLC. The company extends the traditional dinner theatre concept to include not only the dinner and the theatre, but also an opportunity for the audience to participate as performers. In addition, he worked as a semi-professional magician, has taught classes in magic and dulcimer, and has worked as a professional storyteller.

Andersen's feature puzzle/history articles have appeared in *GAMES* magazine for the past fifteen years. Most recently, he has edited pastiches of Sherlock Holmes entitled *The Speckled Band, Author's Expanded Edition* and *The Affairs of Sherlock Holmes*.

More Books from Theme Park Press

Theme Park Press publishes dozens of books each year for Disney fans and for general and academic audiences. Here are just a few of our titles. For the complete catalog, including book descriptions and excerpts, please visit:

ThemeParkPress.com

From Disneyland's
Tom Sawyer
to *Disney Legend*

The Adventures of Tom Nabbe

TOM NABBE

From
Jungle Cruise Skipper
to *Disney Legend*

40 Years of Magical Memories at Disney

William "Sully" Sullivan

It's A
CRAZY BUSINESS

The
GOOFY
Life of a
Disney
Legend

Pinto Colvig
Edited and Introduced by Todd James Pierce

**50 YEARS
IN THE
MOUSE HOUSE**

The Lost Memoir of One of Disney's Nine Old Men

ERIC LARSON
Edited by Didier Ghez and Joe Campana

DISNEY'S GRAND TOUR
WALT AND ROY'S EUROPEAN VACATION
SUMMER 1935

DIDIER GHEZ

EVERYTHING
I KNOW
I LEARNED FROM
DISNEY ANIMATED
FEATURE FILMS
Advice for Living Happily Ever After

JIM KORKIS
Author of
The Vault of Walt

A Disney Historian FUN FACT Book

Great Big
Beautiful
Tomorrow

Walt Disney
and Technology

Christian Moran
with Rolly Crump,
Bob Gurr, Jim Korkis,
Sam Gennawey, and Dr.
Maureen Furniss, Ph.D.

"Prepare to be enchanted, bewildered and mesmerized by this   Guillermo del Toro
beat-by-beat account of the Haunted Mansion's creation."   Award-winning film director

The Unauthorized Story of
Walt Disney's
Haunted Mansion

Jeff Baham

Foreword by Rolly Crump

MOUSE IN TRANSITION

An Insider's Look at
Disney Feature Animation

STEVE HULETT
Foreword by John Musker
Disney Feature Films Animation Director

Who's the Leader of the Club?

Walt Disney's Leadership Lessons

JIM KORKIS
Foreword by Henry Hardt
Professor of Business Law and Professor of Finance
Buena Vista University

LIFE IN THE MOUSE HOUSE

MEMOIR OF A DISNEY STORY ARTIST

HOMER BRIGHTMAN
Edited by Didier Ghez

WINDOW ON MAIN STREET

35 Years of Creating
Happiness at
Disneyland Park

Van Arsdale
France

Founder
and
Professor Emeritus
Disney Universities

Van Arsdale France
Foreword by Dick Nunis
Former Chairman, Walt Disney Attractions